PENGUIN BOOKS

THE MOTHER I NEVER KNEW

Born on 19 August 1950 in Shiggaon, north Karnataka, Sudha Murty is a renowned author, philanthropist, teacher, engineer, visionary and leader. As founder of the Murty Trust, she is dedicated to preserving and celebrating art, cultural heritage, science and research, Indian books and manuscripts, and knowledge systems born in India. Murty's literary works have captured readers' hearts with their simplicity, warmth and insight. From novels and short stories to travelogues, her books have been translated into all major Indian languages, selling over 30 lakh copies around the country. Several of her books have also been translated into Italian and Arabic. Among her most famous titles are *Grandma's Bag of Stories*, *Gently Falls the Bakula*, *Three Thousand Stitches* and *Wise and Otherwise*. Her writings are informed by values of compassion and kindness, in keeping with our culture and heritage. Her non-fiction stories are based on her time at the Infosys Foundation, where she worked with people from all walks of life.

Through the Infosys Foundation, Murty established numerous schools, hospitals and orphanages across India, impacting the lives of thousands of individuals. Over the years, her efforts have been recognized with many honorary doctorates and prestigious awards, including the Padma Bhushan and the Padma Shri from the Government of India in 2023 and 2006, respectively; the R.K. Narayan Award for Literature in 2006; and the Lal Bahadur Shastri National Award in 2020. She was also awarded the Rajyothsava and the Dana Chintamani Attimabbe Award for excellence in Kannada literature by the Government of Karnataka in 2000 and 2012, respectively.

T0148868

SUDHA MURTY

The Mother I Never Knew

Two Novellas

PENGUIN BOOKS

An imprint of Penguin Random House

PENGUIN BOOKS

USA | Canada | UK | Ireland | Australia
New Zealand | India | South Africa | China | Singapore

Penguin Books is part of the Penguin Random House group of companies
whose addresses can be found at global.penguinrandomhouse.com

Published by Penguin Random House India Pvt. Ltd
4th Floor, Capital Tower 1, MG Road,
Gurugram 122 002, Haryana, India

First published by Penguin Books India 2014
This edition published in Penguin Books by Penguin Random House India 2023

ISBN 9780143422259

Typeset in Sabon by R. Ajith Kumar, New Delhi
Printed at Thomson Press India Ltd, New Delhi

www.penguin.co.in

To my friend Lakshmi
for always giving me the right perspective through our
decade-long friendship

Contents

VENKATESH

CONTENTS

MUKESH

Venkatesh

I

Unexpected News

Venkatesh was terribly upset when he found out that he had been transferred to Hubli. He didn't know what he was going to do about it. Absent-mindedly, he started driving towards his house in Jayanagar.

He had known that his transfer was due at the bank, and he would not have minded going to a place nearby like Kanakapura, Kolar or Mysore. But Hubli? It seemed so unfamiliar and distant. The end of summer was pleasantly warm in Bangalore. Who knew how it was in Hubli?

'Maybe I should listen to my colleagues,' he thought. Venkatesh knew that he did not really need a job. His family was healthy and financially sound. His co-workers often remarked that had they been in his shoes, they would have opted for voluntary retirement, but Venkatesh did not like to be idle. His wife, Shanta, ran the house very efficiently and handled the family finances better than an investment banker. So there was nothing for him to do at home either. He was just 'Madam's husband' to the household help who knew that he had no say in any matter.

When he reached home, Shanta was on her way out. He guessed from the fancy clothes that she had a programme at the Ladies' Club. She was proud to be president there. Besides that, she was a member of the college committee and vice president of the school committee while being an active investor in the stock market. She was scarcely at home, and when she was, she was permanently on the phone or the laptop.

Their daughter, Gauri, would often chide her mother, 'Amma, please take your business outside. Your unending telephone calls disturb my study time.'

It always made Shanta angry.

When Venkatesh saw his wife today, he noticed that she had coloured her hair, got a facial and applied make-up. Yet, the lines of age showed distinctly on her face and hands. She was an unabashed show-off and was particularly conscious of her appearance; she was wearing a new white sari with diamond earrings, along with diamond bangles and a diamond necklace. It must be a special occasion to call forth the services of so many diamonds at once, he thought.

Shanta's sharp voice cut through his thoughts, 'I have to see Appa on my way back from the event. Amma isn't feeling very well either. So I'm going to be late. Don't wait for me at dinner.'

She left without waiting for a reply.

Shanta's parents lived nearby in Jayanagar. Though she had asked them to come and live with her, they had not agreed and were adamant about staying at their own place. Her mother had said, 'It is not proper to stay with the son-in-law. If we continue staying in our house, we can keep a distance and be close to you at the same time.'

Shanta had relented but visited them at least once every day despite her busy schedule.

Venkatesh lay down on the sofa. When Gauri came downstairs a few minutes later, she found him deep in thought. She was immediately concerned, 'What's wrong, Anna? Are you feeling unwell?'

He looked at his daughter. Gauri was tall, thin, dusky and attractive. She was a quiet and intelligent girl and Venkatesh loved her with all his heart. 'Gauri, I have been transferred to Hubli,' he said, his voice full of despair.

'So what? Why are you upset? Hubli is not far. If you leave at night, you'll be there by morning. Cheer up, Anna, cheer up.' Gauri was an eternal optimist; she could make anyone feel better.

'You don't understand. I may have to set up house there. The place is new to me and I don't know when I'll be transferred back here . . .'

'Anna, there are two solutions to your problem,' Gauri

interrupted. 'You can ask Amma to use her connections and get the transfer cancelled; or you can go there, stay for a year and try to come back after that.'

Venkatesh did not want to cancel the transfer through unofficial channels. Besides, he knew what his business-minded wife would say: 'Why do you work for such a meagre salary? My manager is paid more than you. Ask for voluntary retirement and relax at home.'

Shanta spoke little, and was always to the point. Sometimes it seemed that she was devoid of all feeling. Her lack of emotion may have been of great help in her business, but how could anyone live life like that?

Venkatesh was feeling hot and decided to shower for the second time in the day. His house was fully equipped with modern amenities—thanks to Shanta and their older child, Ravi. Though Ravi had been young during the construction of the house, he had sat down and discussed everything with his mother.

Ravi was now in America. He had foreseen the business possibilities in computers and majored in computer science. After his engineering studies, he had immediately found a software job and the company had sent him to the USA. He called his mother often to talk to her. 'Times have changed, Amma. Who wants to stay in America permanently? I'll work here for two years and then I'll start my own company in India,' he would say.

'Yes, you must. Don't be foolish like your father

and accept an inconsequential job offer and stick to it. Fortune doesn't tap on everyone's door, you know. Only the courageous and aggressive win Lakshmi over,' Shanta would advise her son.

While showering, Venkatesh heard Gauri laying the table in the next room. He thought of her affectionately. She had been different from Ravi right from her childhood. She thought about the consequences of her actions before doing anything. Gauri had completed her MBBS and was now in the first year of her MD in gynaecology, but her mother was disappointed with her choice of profession. With her intelligence, patience and ability to remain calm in any situation, Gauri would have been very successful had she opted for an MBA. Shanta knew that Ravi planned to own a computer business. She thought that if Gauri also followed Ravi's career path, the family could earn a lot of money.

Shanta had tried hard to convince Gauri after her MBBS, 'Gauri, babies are delivered twenty-four hours a day. You'll never find the time to relax or do anything else. You have studied hard, and invested money and energy. But there is barely any return for the amount of work doctors must do. Listen to me and pursue a business course. If you understand the share business, you can earn many crores within a year with careful investments in the stock market . . .'

'Amma, should I buy a cow just because I have a rope?

I don't understand or like the investment business at all. I want to continue studying medicine right now. I really like it,' Gauri had said.

Shanta had turned to Ravi and grumbled, 'This girl is downright idealistic; it's because she's got everything so easily. She doesn't think about her future or how she will earn money. Instead, she misunderstands whatever I say. If I were also a dreamer like the father and the daughter, both Gauri and you would have been on the streets. Does she realize the effort and sacrifice behind all my achievements? She simply says whatever comes to her mind.'

'Amma, you still don't know what a problem she can be—just wait until she is married,' Ravi had said, provoking his mother further.

'Maybe. Or perhaps her father is supporting her secretly. Otherwise, how can she be so bold?' Shanta had got furious at the thought. But she never expressed her wrath. Business had taught her a big lesson: she should never reveal her true feelings to anyone—not even to her daughter.

Unlike Shanta, Venkatesh was open with Gauri and they often had frank discussions. People frequently commented that in their family, the son took after the mother and the daughter after the father.

Venkatesh stepped out of the bathroom after his shower and donned a thin pyjama and kurta. He entered the dining room and found Gauri pouring watermelon juice into two glasses.

She looked up when he walked in, 'Anna, you look tired. Do you want to eat something?'

Venkatesh smiled and shook his head.

'Do you know why Amma was dressed up today?' she asked.

'I got the impression that there's an event at the Ladies' Club.'

'Yes, there is an important meeting at the club this evening. But the interesting news is that Mrs Veena Purushottam is going to preside over it. You must have heard of her, haven't you?'

'Yes, I have. She's one of the richest socialite Kannadigas in Bangalore and usually makes an appearance in high-profile meetings, functions and parties. But I don't understand why it's interesting news . . .'

'Oh Anna, you're such a simple person! Veena has a daughter of marriageable age. Her name is Priyanka—but most people call her Pinki. Amma is looking for a suitable match for Ravi and she thinks that Pinki is perfect. So she is trying to impress Veena.'

Venkatesh fell silent. He thought, 'When it comes to Ravi, Shanta never thinks of asking for my opinion. It is better to discuss these things together as a family. While love marriage is a different matter, much forethought and conversation are necessary in arranged marriages. It is better to select the daughter-in-law from a stratum lower than the groom's. If the girl is from a family richer than ours, then perhaps Ravi's life may also turn out to be like mine.'

Venkatesh felt sad and for a few minutes, he was worried about his son. But almost instantly, he knew that Ravi could handle things better than he had.

Gauri read her father's mind. 'Anna, what are you thinking about? Is it Ravi? Please don't worry about him. I promise you that whenever I get married, it'll be according to your wish. I'm not saying that I'll marry the boy you choose, but I'll discuss it with you and I'll obtain your consent. Ravi is different. Let Amma and Ravi decide about his marriage. Forget about it,' she said.

She changed the subject, 'Anna, you really don't seem to be yourself today. Come, let's go to Lalbagh for a walk. It's not healthy for you to mope around at home and do nothing, especially in the evenings.'

Ever since he could remember, Venkatesh had taken Gauri for walks in Lalbagh. Today, she was the one taking him. Without giving him a chance to refuse, she brought the car keys and dragged him to the garage.

While reversing the car, Venkatesh looked at the family home. It was a beautiful house with a beautiful name—'Anandita'. Built on almost ten thousand square feet of land, the house had a garden in the front with a long driveway that would allow at least three or four cars at a time. The flooring of the house was in marble. There were four bedrooms with attached toilets, teakwood doors, ultra-modern facilities, and separate quarters for the domestic help; the Gurkha watchman took care of the garden, and Nanjappa and Chikkavva handled the household chores. Besides free accommodation and food, they were paid a monthly salary of seven thousand rupees each. They were content and went about their work happily, leaving nothing for Shanta to do.

Venkatesh knew that to any observer, their family would appear perfect. And yet, there was heaviness in his heart—something was definitely amiss.

2

A Difference of Opinion

As he drove to Lalbagh with Gauri sitting by his side, Venkatesh was drawn into the past and his marriage to Shanta.

His wife was the only child of her parents born after many, many years. Her parents, Suryanarayana Rao and Savitramma, had made special offerings to Lord Manjunatha of Dharmasthala and performed Naga Puja at Vidurashwatha before her mother finally conceived. Savitramma had wanted to name her daughter Nagalakshmi, but Rao decided to call her Shanta after his mother.

Suryanarayana's employment in the government revenue department had several perks that surpassed his regular salary. Cereals, vegetables, oils and butter—everything was abundant and free. Government peons worked at his home and took care of the family's needs. So Shanta grew up like a princess with her parents fulfilling all her demands. Her studies progressed and the family was transferred to bigger towns and cities until they finally ended up in Bangalore, where Shanta graduated with a Bachelor of Arts from Maharani's College.

In the old days, most government employees in Bangalore resided in areas like Basavanagudi, Gandhi Bazaar, NR Colony, Malleshwaram, Sriramapura and Rajajinagar. However, Suryanarayana had decided to rent a house in Chamrajpet and buy a site in Jayanagar, which was a developing suburb that was still largely a forested area. People told him that it was absolute foolishness to buy anything there, but Suryanarayana did not care and bought the site anyway.

Meanwhile, he also became a member of the Basavanagudi Club. It was there that he met J.M. Rao or JMR—a Class 1 officer in the Indian Railways. During his tenure in pre-Partition India, JMR had been transferred to different places in the country—along with the relocations came the freebies of being a Class 1 officer: free housing, multiple servants and free railway passes—before buying a home in Basavanagudi and settling down in Bangalore.

Shrewd Suryanarayana took an instant liking to JMR and his small family—an aged mother, a wife and a son, Venkatesh, of marriageable age. JMR's mother Champakka was a loud-mouthed old woman who had become a widow when she was twenty. From that day on, she had lived solely for the sake of her son and he had become the centre of her life. A tough life had ensured that she was no less than a tigress protecting her cubs. Unlike her, JMR's wife Indiramma was so quiet and submissive that people often noticed this and commented upon it. Even JMR, known for his strictness in the office, was meek at home in his mother's presence. Champakka happily ruled the roost and saved enough money from JMR's income. Upon retirement, JMR contributed money from his provident fund to buy the family two large sites in Basavanagudi in addition to their current home in the same area.

Suryanarayana thought, 'Venkatesh has a good job at the State Bank of India here in Bangalore. If Shanta gets married to him, she will stay in the same city and we can see her frequently. Besides, Venkatesh is an only child and we won't have to worry about sharing JMR's inheritance later. Old Champakka is stubborn, I know, but she is already past eighty. How much longer can she live? Indiramma is quite dumb and Shanta can easily handle her. Yes, Venkatesh is a good match for my daughter.'

Suryanarayana developed a close friendship with JMR very quickly and broached the subject of marriage within a few months. Old Champakka immediately approved of Shanta because she too was the only child of rich parents. A grand wedding was held; nobody cared to ask Venkatesh or Indiramma for an opinion.

Suryanarayana was right about Champakka. Within a year of her grandson's marriage, she breathed her last in her sleep. The captain of the ship was no more.

A few months later, Venkatesh was transferred to Mysore. That's where Ravi was born. When the family returned to Bangalore a year later, Indiramma suddenly died of a heart attack. Soon after, JMR had a stroke that left him bedridden, paralysed and unable to speak. However, Shanta did not have to attend to him for more than a few months. Just as Suryanarayana had started to worry about Shanta's fate in case the old man lived long in that condition, JMR too passed away. Thus, Shanta became the sole mistress of the house within three years of her marriage and Suryanarayana became the most senior member of the family.

Venkatesh's musings came to a halt as the car reached Lalbagh and Gauri remarked, 'Anna, see how crowded it has become these days.'

Yes, Lalbagh was very crowded. Many people came to exercise there. It was no longer meant just for young lovers and old people. Venkatesh replied, 'Isn't it natural? I used to come alone before, and now, you're with me. That makes two of us. The population has definitely grown.'

The road near the west gate was convenient for a stroll and quiet too. Venkatesh and Gauri walked along the cement footpath in the cool and pleasant evening breeze. 'Anna, you have travelled quite a lot. What made you settle down in Bangalore?' Gauri asked.

'Well, I've been told that the letter J in Father's name stands for Joshi and that we are from some village in the Mysore state. But I really don't know much else and I don't think that Father did either. So we adopted any place that we stayed in and we happened to like this city.'

'But why do we have so few relatives from your side of the family? Everybody I know is from Amma's side. Where are your cousins, uncles and aunts?'

'You see, Grandma struggled to raise my father and none of her relatives helped or visited her during that time. So when we became wealthy, Grandma didn't want us to go see our cousins or their families.'

'Okay, I can understand that.' Gauri paused. 'But what about your mother's relatives?'

'You must understand, child; my mother was innocent and meek, but she was also very intelligent. Often, you remind me of her. The only difference is that you speak your mind, but she couldn't. Those days were like that. In the end, Grandma reigned supreme in the family and Mother spent all her time knitting, embroidering, painting and indulging in other such creative activities.'

'Anna, why didn't you ever argue with your Grandma?'

Venkatesh said sadly, 'For the same reason that you don't argue with your mother. It's because some people are approachable and some are not. My Grandma and your mother belong to the latter category. It's no use talking to them; it's like breaking our heads against a wall. Their decision is final—whether right or wrong. We simply choose to stay quiet to keep the peace.'

Engrossed in conversation, the father–daughter duo realized that they had already completed one round along the pond. Avoiding the crowded road in front of the Glass House, they turned back on the same path.

'Anna, maybe things would have been different had Amma stayed at home,' Gauri said, thinking of her busy mother.

'Perhaps, but the truth is that we'll never know. Initially, Shanta was a homemaker. When Amma and Appa passed away, I had to take responsibility for my family and the inheritance I received.'

'Grandfather came to your help then, didn't he?'

'Yes, he did.' Venkatesh recalled. 'Your grandfather Suryanarayana is a smart man. He made me take a loan from the bank I worked in and helped us to construct two commercial buildings—Ganga–Tunga—on the Basavanagudi site. Your mother sold our home in the area and we shifted to Jayanagar. Though the land and the money were mine, your grandfather was the mastermind behind the plan. He advised us to rent out both the buildings to private companies. Even in those days, we immediately started earning a profit of three lakh rupees per month after the loan instalment payments. Within fifteen years, the loan was easily cleared. Now, a software start-up has taken the buildings on lease and we get twenty lakhs every month.'

Gauri interrupted, 'That is a lot of money.'

'Yes, but your grandfather didn't just stop there. After the buildings had been rented out, he assisted us with our investments in the beginning, and I was surprised to see your Amma take to the business of investing like a duck to water. Over the years, her investments have returned more than ten times the original money and she's bought new properties.' Venkatesh didn't tell Gauri that except for the Ganga–Tunga buildings, none of the new properties were in his name; they were in the names of Ravi, Gauri and Shanta.

'If we have so many good investments, then why doesn't Amma take it easy?' asked Gauri.

'Why don't I give up my job at the bank too? At first, earning money was a necessity, but now working has become a habit. It's not that your mother needs the money; her work really seems to give her immense satisfaction. That's why she does what she does.'

For years now, Shanta had never asked Venkatesh about his salary. She didn't care; she had much more money coming in. But the truth was that Shanta had never really worked hard in her life. Her strengths were her common sense and her sound knowledge of business, both perhaps inherited from her father. It wasn't child's play to amass wealth by investing in the stock market. While some became rich, others were completely ruined.

'Anna, what do you think of Veena and Purushottam? They may become our relatives some day.'

'What can I say, Gauri? I barely know them. From what I've seen, their social work is restricted to the city—they distribute food to children in the slums or give speeches about children's welfare while ensuring media coverage in newspapers and television. All their activities seem publicity-oriented. I'm not sure if they are genuinely concerned about social issues or helping people in other cities or villages.'

'But even social work has become commercial these days,' Gauri remarked.

'Yes, I know. I worry that a girl from such a family may not have integrity or dedication towards her work.'

'That's what you think, Anna. I'm quite sure that Amma and Ravi think differently.'

They walked in silence for a few minutes. The sky was getting dark when they reached the car and started on their way home. Venkatesh's thoughts returned to his transfer. He could quit his job. But what would he do at home anyway?

~

A few hours later, the pleasant evening had turned into a warm night. Shanta turned on the air conditioning and thought about the meeting at the club that evening. She had praised Veena very carefully while introducing her. Veena had looked pleased after that. Their meeting was so professional; it was like one businessman meeting another. One daughter. One son. Shanta knew that Veena was thinking along the same lines, but they were both too clever to say anything directly.

Shanta lay down on the bed and thought of her potential daughter-in-law. Was she beautiful? What would Veena and her husband give their daughter Pinki for the wedding? Shanta had heard that Pinki had studied fashion designing—a modern discipline. 'Will she be able to find a job easily, or will she have to start something of her own? It's important for us to know. How will it help Ravi's start-up?' she thought.

She tried to sleep but couldn't. She turned to her side and saw Venkatesh sleeping blissfully. By this time, she knew about his transfer to Hubli. 'It's no use telling him anything,' she said to herself. 'He will hate it if I tell him to quit his job, the job that barely pays him. I'll never understand why—is it wrong to want to earn money? Or is he jealous that his wife earns more than he does? Maybe all Indian men think that the wife should work, but her income should not exceed her husband's. She must be educated, but less than her husband. The wife may be an equal, but not higher than that.'

Disturbed, sleep drifted further away from her. When

Shanta had married Venkatesh, the house in Basavanagudi was already very old. The family lived a simple life on a tight budget under Champakka's watchful eye. 'There's such a big difference between those days and today,' Shanta thought.

But a glance at her husband made her feel sad. He'd never understood her or helped with the business. When his father died he had not left a will, but Venkatesh had inherited everything since he was the only heir. Unfortunately, he had no idea of his father's finances. When they opened the bank locker after JMR's death, both Suryanarayana and Shanta were shocked. The locker was filled with gold which had a thin layer of fungus on top since it had been lying unused for years. The gold itself was worth lakhs of rupees even in those times, and yet the family had lived a miserly life.

'But even then, our status in society and the changes in our lives weren't achieved overnight; I have toiled day and night to achieve all this single-handedly,' she thought proudly.

For a moment, Shanta envied Pinki, 'Everything that I have struggled to earn will go to my daughter-in-law one day. My darling son Ravi will also belong to that girl. Maybe I should share my concerns with Venkatesh. Or maybe I shouldn't. He won't understand anyway.'

There was still no sign of sleep despite the cool air conditioning. So she tried to think of solutions, 'If the girl is obedient, she can be controlled. But that's so difficult these days. Also, I'm sure that Veena's daughter won't be submissive. Let's see what happens when the time comes.'

The cuckoo clock chimed 3 a.m. Ravi had gifted her the clock last year when she was in Switzerland for her birthday. Her heart filled with love and pride as she thought of him and, finally, she fell asleep.

The next morning Shanta slept in later than usual. When she came out from the shower, both Venkatesh and Gauri were ready to leave for the day—her husband for the office, and her daughter for college. Shanta sat down at the dining table and sipped her tea. She waited for them to mention the transfer as she stared at the headlines in the newspaper.

Venkatesh said, 'I'll be leaving for Hubli this week. The head office said that I should be back in Bangalore after six months.'

He didn't ask her to come. She didn't offer to go either. 'Where will you stay?'

Gauri interrupted, 'My friend Sunita Patil's parents live in Hubli. I contacted them and they've promised to make some arrangement for six months.'

'So that's it. Father and daughter have already sorted things out,' thought Shanta.

Just then, the household help Nanjappa called out, 'Amma, there's a phone call from Ravi Sir.'

Shanta forgot about everything and ran to the telephone.

3

A New City

A few days later, Gauri accompanied her father to the railway station to say goodbye. Shanta had already bid him farewell at home; she had a meeting with the auditors. 'See you soon,' she told him. 'Call me later. Remember—I can always arrange for your transfer back to Bangalore.'

Venkatesh was booked in a first-class compartment in Kittur Express. He was carrying a duffel bag with only three changes of clothes since he was planning to return to Bangalore that same weekend.

When they reached the station, Gauri was happy to see that many of her father's friends and co-workers had also come to say goodbye. They seemed to have genuine affection and regard for her father.

Venkatesh was very friendly and helpful at work. He actively participated in celebrations such as Ganesh

Chaturthi, Dussehra, Kannada Rajyotsava and Ugadi. Once, a clerk called Geeta had been on maternity leave. When she came back to work after four months, she tearfully confided in him, 'Sir, I have to go and be with the baby after 1 p.m. because there's no one at home after that time.' Venkatesh told her that she could take short-term leave without pay, but Geeta was not ready to do that because she had to make loan payments. So Venkatesh accommodated her request. He told her, 'You may leave early and I'll manage the counter in your absence.'

During another incident, Mahesh was handling the cash counter and found that somebody had erroneously paid a thousand rupees in excess. Everybody wanted to celebrate and have a party with the money, but Venkatesh disagreed, 'No, that's not right. Let's keep it aside. We'll return it if the owner comes looking for it.' When nobody came to claim the money, it was given away to the office watchman Karim for his wife's C-section operation.

Thus, Venkatesh had become quite popular in the office. Most people were sad to see him go. The few colleagues who envied him would talk behind his back and say that any man could be generous if his wife made so much money. But to his face, they'd praise him. Venkatesh was aware of the criticism, but he always let it go.

At the station, Mahesh told Venkatesh, 'Sir, once you go to Hubli, people there may not let you come back here quickly. Please don't stay on there, Sir.'

Venkatesh settled down at the window seat of the compartment and replied, 'No, I won't. I can't. My Gauri is in the final year of her studies. I don't know where she'll go after that. It's not difficult to stay away from Bangalore, but it's almost impossible to stay away from her.'

He looked fondly at Gauri. Her tears, suppressed till now, flowed freely down her cheeks. Her father was her true friend. He had been transferred frequently in the past, but it was always to nearby places so that he could come back home at night. This was the first time he was going to be away for this long.

'Anna, take care of your health. Sunita's father will come to the station to pick you up . . .' The train started moving as Gauri was speaking to her father; everyone waved goodbye.

After the platform vanished from Venkatesh's sight, he looked around his compartment and thought, 'I should be back in six months. I don't think I'll use this train more than half a dozen times.'

He had no idea that his life's foundation would be thoroughly shaken in six months.

When the train arrived in Hubli at five o'clock the next morning, the sky was still dark. The passengers were grumbling, 'The train has arrived before schedule and now it's going to be hard to find an autorickshaw.'

The ticket collector opened the door and asked all the passengers to disembark.

As soon as Venkatesh alighted from the train, his Hubli colleagues came forward with garlands and bouquets to welcome him. They introduced themselves almost in unison.

'Sir, I'm Chimmanakatti, the cashier.'

'I am Kamalakkanavar, the office assistant.'

'Sir, I'm Rotti, the clerk.'

Venkatesh was taken aback. What strange names!

Suddenly he heard a hoarse voice, 'Sir, I am Anant Patil, Sunita's father. My daughter called me last night and told me your train timings. Please come with me.'

Then he turned to the others and announced, 'Your saheb is coming to my house in Vishweshwar Nagar. He will freshen up there and then I'll bring him to the office at 10 a.m.'

Quickly, he dispersed the crowd and asked Venkatesh to follow him with a wave of his hand.

Anant Patil was a fat, charming and friendly man. On the way to his house, Venkatesh was fascinated by Hubli's narrow and heavily crowded lanes. Soon, Anant started talking about his family. 'Sir, I work in the Public Works Department of the government and I am close to my retirement. I have a son, Naveen, and a daughter, Sunita, who is Gauri's classmate in Bangalore Medical College.'

Venkatesh could barely understand what he was saying. Though Patil was speaking Kannada, the north Karnataka dialect sounded quite unfamiliar.

A short while later, they reached Patil's two-bedroom house in Vishweshwar Nagar. The adjoining single-bedroom home also belonged to him. There was a grove in front of the house with tulsi, champak and coconut trees. Patil's wife, Vijayabai, invited them in with a smile, 'Please come in and have some tea.' She looked at Venkatesh and added, 'Then you can take a short nap. You've probably not slept well in the train.'

Venkatesh was hesitant, 'No, I don't need to sleep. I'll drink tea and then go to the office guest house.'

'Oh, please don't stay in the guest house. Think of our home as your own. Sunita tells us so much about yours.'

'What has she told you?'

Patil immediately said, 'She says that she meets you for lunch almost every week when she visits Gauri. Sometimes, when there's no water in the hostel, she goes to your house for her shower too. Gauri is extremely generous and brings her a lot of home-made food and snacks. So how can we let you stay in the guest house? It wouldn't be right.'

His outburst reminded Venkatesh of the roaring Jog Falls and he smiled.

Patil's wife scolded her husband, 'Please lower your volume. Mother-in-law is asleep in the next room.'

At 9.30 a.m. they ate breakfast, and then Patil dropped Venkatesh at his office and told him firmly, 'You must come home right after office hours. Here's my address.'

The State Bank of India office was in Keshwapur close

to the railway station. Venkatesh learnt the workings of the bank and had lunch with some of his office colleagues. He tasted Dharwad food for the first time. His palate was accustomed to Mysore cuisine thanks to his mother Indiramma. In the afternoon, he went to the office guest house. He didn't like it at all. He thought, 'It's going to be hard to stay here for six months. Also, the work in the office is less than half of what I had in Bangalore and I'll have plenty of free time. What will I do? How will I spend the whole day in the office here?'

That night, he dined with the Patils. Vijayabai had made *ranjaka*, sambar, stuffed *baingan* bhaji and chapattis. She asked him, 'How do you like the food here?'

'It's good.'

Anant Patil laughed, 'You will say it's good even if it's not. Tell me the truth, do you really like it?'

Venkatesh repeated his answer.

Patil told him, 'Sir, the one-bedroom house adjacent to ours is vacant right now. My son, Naveen, and his wife, Rekha, were staying there. I preferred that they lived separately so that they could have their privacy and still be close to us. Unfortunately, many factories in Hubli are shutting down. Despite being a mechanical engineer, Naveen did a course in computers and now works in Pune. Even though I wish he were here, what can I do? He's my only son. I want him to be happy wherever he is.'

Venkatesh, too, felt sad at the thought of people being

forced to migrate to other cities with the closing down of industries.

'So you are welcome to stay in our house next door. It's independent and has a telephone. You can have your meals with us too, or we can arrange to get you breakfast and dinner from outside if you prefer. Please choose whatever you are comfortable with. We have no problems at all,' Patil was direct and straightforward.

'I'll think about it,' replied Venkatesh.

A few days later, he became Patil's tenant.

~

A month went by and Venkatesh settled into a routine.

Patil's house was always crowded with friends and relatives. Venkatesh often wondered how the couple managed to entertain everybody.

It was a typical patriarchal family and the women were busy cooking and making jowar rotis the whole day. They barely emerged from the kitchen. There was plenty of avalakki or puffed rice kept in tins for snack-time.

Venkatesh couldn't help thinking about Shanta. Had she been placed in such circumstances, she would have rebelled. Her mind was on things beyond the home—which property is for sale, which of the equities will be more profitable? Ever since her first successful stint in the stock market, she had not entered the kitchen, nor did anyone expect her to. Ravi would often tell his mother, 'Amma, don't waste your time with household chores. Hire somebody to take care of them. Your time is precious.'

Venkatesh wondered, 'Does anyone ever say that to Vijayabai?'

Soon, Venkatesh became an intimate member of their family. Patil and he would sit in the courtyard every evening and chat.

One Monday evening, Patil said, 'Rao ji, I have a younger brother, Dinesh. When we sit and talk, we lose track of time. The tired women would leave tea and milk powder out for us and go to bed. We would make our own tea and continue chatting.'

'Where is he now?'

Patil took a deep breath, 'He's in Mumbai and I really miss him. I was raised in a joint family. We are the Patils of Kallapur. It is a village close to Hubli and our house always had at least twenty people living in it at any time. But that's enough about me. What about your family, Sir?'

'Ours is a very small family,' Venkatesh said. 'I am an only son. My father was transferred frequently and I really don't remember meeting any relatives. My parents never talked about them either. Sometimes, I wish that I also had affectionate brothers like you. Where do all your other relatives stay?'

'Our relatives are spread everywhere. That reminds me—the thread ceremony of my Aunt's grandson is on

Sunday, in Shiggaon. I want you to see the customs and traditions of our region. Let's go together next weekend.'

'But I don't know them,' said Venkatesh.

'Rao ji, it's different here. You don't have to wait for a personal invitation. Simply come with me. Just like Bangalore has many neighbouring places that are worth visiting—such as Belur, Halebidu and Mysore—we also have nice places around Hubli. There's Gadag, Koliwada, Savanur and Shishunal. We must go visit all of them. After all, you are only going to be here for six months.'

Venkatesh nodded. That sounded nice. He had already been to Bangalore three times. Everyone was busy there. Ravi was back from America and the search for a suitable girl was duly in progress. Gauri was preoccupied with studying for her exams. Still, she called up her father often and told him repeatedly, 'Anna, you must take a break from work and be here with me during my exams. If I get a few holidays for preparatory leave, I will also come to Hubli.'

4

A Case of Mistaken Identity

The summer had ended and it was the month of Shravana. The rain had washed the muddy roads of Hubli when Venkatesh set out for Shiggaon with Anant Patil. It was an hour's journey from Hubli. When they reached Shiggaon, the pond outside the village was filled with water and there was greenery all around. The thread ceremony was in Deshpande Galli, thus named because all the residents in the lane were Deshpandes.

When Venkatesh stepped through the gates of the big ancestral house called *wade*, he noticed that the walls were at least eighteen inches thick and made of clay. There was a huge courtyard inside the house. The teakwood pillars and the ceilings had delicate carvings in the wood. 'This is so different from our Jayanagar bungalow back home,' he thought.

In Bangalore, it was almost mandatory to hire a big hall for such celebrations. But here, the ceremony was in the family home.

Finally, Venkatesh spotted the boy or *vatu*, whose thread ceremony was taking place. He was eight years old. His head was shaved except for a little pigtail in the centre of his head.

Anant Patil said, 'Since the ceremony was in the family house, we didn't even print invitation cards, Rao ji. We went from home to home and personally invited people. Tell me, what do you think of my ancestral home?'

'It's really nice,' replied Venkatesh, looking around. He noticed that Patil's relatives were still coming in. It seemed like he knew everyone in north Karnataka.

'There should be around two hundred people here today,' Patil said modestly.

'Please go ahead and meet your friends and relatives.' Venkatesh felt like an outsider, despite the warmth of the people around. He added, 'Meanwhile, I'll take a look around and see the market.'

Patil laughed, 'Our whole Shiggaon is just about one round. Please eat some *chakkali* and drink some tea. I will accompany you too.'

While they were talking, banana leaves had been spread in a line on the floor. People sat down and were served chakkali, *avalakki* and *besan* laddu. Sensing his opportunity, Venkatesh slipped out of the house and went into the streets. He had not had a chance to buy a gift for the boy. So he asked an old man on the road, 'Sir, is there a jewellery store nearby?'

'Yes, there is. It's in the centre of Shiggaon and is located near the old hospital. Bannabhatta's house is also close to it. The shop belongs to Krishnachari.'

Venkatesh was confused. The landmarks didn't make any sense to him at all. He walked further and that's when he realized that all the shops were located on one long street—just like Brigade Road in Bangalore. Everything was available on this road.

Within a few minutes, he found the shop. It was tiny and had a handwritten board displayed outside: 'Shri Vishwakarma Namah, Sneha Jewellers, Proprietor Krishnachari'. He knocked at the door. An elderly man opened it and said, 'Come in, Master, why are you standing outside?'

'Why is he calling me Master?' Venkatesh wondered. For a second, he thought that the man was talking to someone standing behind him. But when he turned around, there was nobody there.

The man repeated, 'Master, please come in and sit down. I'll be back in two minutes.'

Venkatesh entered the shop. There was an old desk in a corner, an old carpet on the floor and a weighing scale in a glass box standing on the counter. The words 'Shubha Labha' and a swastika mark were displayed on the wall and a framed cross-stitched picture of Balakrishna was hanging next to it. The whole place appeared ancient, especially compared to Krishniah Chetty's stylish shop on Bangalore's busy Commercial Street.

Soon, the man came out of a room. He looked like he was around seventy years old. He took his time rearranging his dhoti and glasses. Then he looked at Venkatesh and said, 'Master, have you fixed your daughter's marriage?'

'What? Whose daughter?' asked Venkatesh.

The man adjusted his glasses and peered at him, 'Your daughter Mandakini. I don't understand. Why are you looking at me like that? Haven't you seen me before?'

'I think you are mistaken. I am not Master and my daughter's name is not Mandakini.'

Immediately, Krishnachari corrected himself, 'I'm sorry, Sir, I mistook you for Shankar Master. I haven't seen him for a long time. So I think I got confused. But . . . is he related to you?'

'I don't have any relatives in this area,' said Venkatesh firmly. He changed the subject, 'I've come to your shop to buy a silver glass. Do you have any?'

'Yes, yes, of course. What's your budget?'

'Around five hundred rupees.'

'All right, let me show you what I have.'

Krishnachari opened an antique wooden box and took out three silver glasses wrapped in an old cloth. There really weren't many options. While Venkatesh was trying to make his choice, Krishnachari observed him keenly. After Venkatesh had picked one and paid for it, the shop owner asked him again, 'May I ask where you've come from? There's an uncanny resemblance between Master and you.'

'I'm from Bangalore.' Venkatesh didn't want to answer any more questions and swiftly exited the shop.

Krishnachari kept looking at him as he walked away.

When Venkatesh returned to the Deshpande mansion, banana leaves were already laid out for lunch. Anant Patil caught him the moment he saw him, 'Where have you been? Everyone is waiting for you. Come, let's eat and leave. It looks like it's about to rain heavily.'

Venkatesh nodded and went to meet the vatu. The boy was sweating profusely and was surrounded by a lot of guests. Venkatesh waited his turn and presented the boy with the silver glass. After that, he joined Patil for lunch.

As they were walking out of the gate after their meal, someone patted Venkatesh on the back and said, 'Shankar, let's go to Kundagola together this year.'

Venkatesh turned around to see a stranger in a white kurta and dhoti. The man's lips were red because of the paan in his mouth.

'I'm sorry, I think you have the wrong man. I have never been to Kundagola.'

Before he could even complete his sentence, the man retorted, 'Shankar, don't give me any excuses. Don't come if you don't want to—or are you still angry with me?'

'You don't understand. I am not Shankar.'

Anant Patil also tried to correct him, 'Parappa, do you know who he is? This gentleman is the new manager of State Bank of India in Hubli. He's staying with us. I think you've had too much tobacco this morning and it has gone to your head.'

Then Patil turned to Venkatesh and said, 'Rao ji, please don't misunderstand him. He must be intoxicated. This man is very fond of Hindustani music, especially if it's the Kirana gharana. He visits Kundagola every year for the music festival.'

Parappa was still staring at Venkatesh in disbelief. Finally, he said, 'I swear that he looks exactly like Shankar Master. Now that I see him closely, I find that Shankar Master looks a little older. Still, both of them are so alike that they could almost be twins. Rao ji, please forgive me.'

Venkatesh nodded. Distracted, he walked towards Patil's car and soon they were on their way back to Hubli. Venkatesh felt uneasy. He asked Patil, 'The people in Shiggaon mistook me for Shankar Master not once, but twice. Who is this man?'

Patil laughed, 'Who knows? My mother says that everyone in this world has six lookalikes. I believe that mine are in other countries, because I haven't met anybody here who looks like me. Maybe your lookalike is right here in this district.'

Days passed and Venkatesh forgot about the incident. A short while later, it was time for the annual Ganesh festival. He was surprised to notice that the celebrations in Hubli surpassed even those in Bangalore. Every street had a Ganesh. Each Ganesh wore different clothes from diverse backgrounds—there was a Ganesh from Kargil, a military Ganesh, a computer-operating Ganesh and a guitar-playing Ganesh.

Patil insisted, 'Rao ji, please don't go to Bangalore for the Ganesh festival. It is worth seeing it here in Hubli. I'd love to take you to Idagunji and Sonda. You may never get such an opportunity again.'

Gauri also thought that it was a good idea and encouraged him to go. Her exams were near and she rarely called him now. However, Shanta phoned him and said, 'You should come back soon. We have to choose a girl for Ravi and we can't do it until you come home.'

Venkatesh knew that that was not true. He replied, 'Perhaps the girl has already been chosen?'

'No, of course not. How can we choose a girl without you? Besides, Ravi is busy these days. He's travelling to Singapore next week. Can you please buy two Dharwad saris and bring them whenever you come to Bangalore? I'd like a black or blue sari with a red border and a light green sari with a dark green border.'

The colour combinations confused Venkatesh. He rarely went shopping, so he asked a lady colleague for guidance.

She told him, 'Sir, you can go to Babu's shop in Broadway or to Gangavati's shop in Dajibanpet. You'll definitely get these combinations there.'

Venkatesh thanked her and went straight to Babu's shop in Broadway. A stranger came up to him and said, 'Master, please keep my bag with you for a few minutes while you are here. I'm going to the shop next door and will be back shortly.'

The man left without waiting for an answer.

Venkatesh was puzzled. He had never met the man before. Who knew what the bag contained? Maybe it was a bomb, or even stolen goods. Was somebody playing games with him? He became tense and worried. Unable to contain himself any longer, he opened the bag and browsed through it. To his surprise, he found green chillies and a bar of butter. Relieved, he kept the bag aside and continued shopping. At the cash counter, he told the salesman, 'Please give this bag to the man who comes looking for Shankar Master.'

One thing was certain—there was a 'Shankar Master' around who resembled him. One person may have made a mistake, but three? Venkatesh was curious.

5

The Meeting

A few weeks after the visit to Shiggaon, Vijayabai insisted on taking Venkatesh to the mutt in Sonda. The Sonda Vadiraja Mutt is one of the eight mutts of Udupi. It is the only mutt located close to Hubli and is revered as the sacred place where the great saint Vadiraja entered his tomb alive.

Anant Patil happily agreed to his wife's request and the three of them started for Sonda on a Saturday. The car ride was simply wonderful. There was lush green everywhere and they stopped to see the *bakula* flowers and *elaichi* bananas in Yellapura, and the Marikamba Temple in Sirsi. They reached their destination around lunchtime.

Venkatesh, Anant Patil and Vijayabai took a room in the mutt. They washed and changed and then seated themselves in the large hall, where there was already a long queue for lunch. Patil and Vijayabai met some family friends and Venkatesh found himself alone. He went and sat down. There was an old woman next to him who asked, 'When did you come here, Shankar?'

Venkatesh wasn't surprised by the mistaken identity any more. Now, he was determined to find more information about his lookalike. He calmly replied, 'I'm not Shankar, but I've heard that I look like him. If I may ask, who are you?'

'I am Manda Aunty from Hulgur. Shankar, I know that we are meeting after a long time. Stop teasing me.'

'Amma, I'm telling you the truth. I am not Shankar.'

She stared at him, 'But you look just like him. His mother Bhagavva and I are good friends.'

'Tell me more. What does Shankar do?'

'He is a primary school teacher and works in Shishunal. He has three daughters—Mandakini, Alakananda and Sarayu.'

'And where does he live?' Venkatesh asked politely.

The old woman was happy to talk to him. She replied, 'Well, he lives in Divate chawl near the Ganesh Talkies movie theatre in Hubli. Shankar also has a house in Shishunal.'

'I don't understand, Amma. Does he live in both places?'

'How do I explain this?' she paused. 'Shankar's mother, Bhagavva, is old and lives in Shishunal with her son while Mangalabai—Shankar's wife—lives in Hubli with the children. The second and third daughters are in college while the oldest daughter Mandakini stays at home and takes tuitions at people's houses.'

The old woman took a long breath and continued, 'That makes Shankar the only earning member of the family. They have no land and barely any money. He's had a tough life. His daughter Mandakini was born in *mulanakshatra*. Her horoscope advises that she should be wedded into a house without a father-in-law. Unfortunately, Shankar is finding it difficult to find a suitable match since he can't afford to pay dowry either. That's why I thought that Shankar had come here to pray for Mandakini.'

Just then, Anant and Vijayabai came back and joined them for lunch, which was served a few minutes later. Venkatesh pondered, 'Shankar has a home in Hubli. I can easily go and meet him. Should I take Patil with me? No, it wouldn't be right. I think I'll go alone.'

~

A few days later, Venkatesh made his way to Divate chawl in Hubli. He located the chawl easily; it was home to at least a dozen families. The mud walls were discoloured and it was obvious that they hadn't been whitewashed for years. Venkatesh found it difficult to enter the chawl because the lane was very narrow. So he parked his car and walked inside. On the way, he passed a water tap and four public toilets.

'Maybe I shouldn't have come,' Venkatesh thought. 'But now that I'm here, I'll finish what I have begun. First, I have to find Shankar's home.'

Luckily for him, he walked a few steps further and saw a door with something scribbled on it. He went closer and saw what was written: 'Shankar Master, Primary School Teacher'.

This was it.

Venkatesh knocked firmly. 'Who is it?' asked a woman's voice.

'Is Master at home?'

'No, he's out. Who are you?' she asked.

'I'm Venkatesh.'

'Well, I'm here. The door is not locked. Please open it and come in. You can sit down and wait. Master should be back soon.'

'Perhaps that's Mangalabai,' Venkatesh thought. He pushed the door open and walked through a small veranda leading to a main hall. Venkatesh sat down and looked around. The only other room was a kitchen. There were unmistakable signs of poverty everywhere—minimal cheap furniture and faded photographs of children were displayed in broken photo-frames. His eyes wandered to Shankar Master's wedding picture; his own photo at that age was identical.

Suddenly, the door opened. An attractive and fair-skinned girl walked in, 'When did you come, Appa? Why are you sitting here all alone?' she smiled and stood in front of him.

She was around Gauri's age, but fairer. She almost looked like Gauri when she smiled. It took her a few seconds to realize her mistake. Venkatesh spoke immediately, 'I'm not your father. My name is Venkatesh and I am a manager in State Bank of India.'

'Sorry Sir, you looked exactly like my father for a moment.'

'What's your name?' he asked her gently.

'Mandakini,' she said and kept standing.

'So she's the one Shankar is worried about,' Venkatesh thought.

'Sir, whom do you want to meet?' Mandakini asked him. 'You see, if you've come to find out about tuitions, then I'm the one to talk to but if you've come to meet my father, you'll have to wait a bit.'

'I want to talk to you. How much have you studied, child?'

'I have passed my Bachelor of Science with a first class. These days, I go to people's houses and teach children.'

'Have you applied for any jobs?'

'Yes, I have applied for both private and government jobs. Right now, I am awaiting the results. Unfortunately, fresher recruitment has decreased now, hasn't it, Sir?' the girl asked.

'Manda, who are you speaking to?' a voice came from the kitchen.

Before she could respond, the main door opened and Shankar Master came in. He saw Venkatesh and stopped in his tracks—shocked at seeing an exact replica of himself. Venkatesh was fascinated too. He stood up. They had the same colour of skin and the same nose, eyes and face. Even their mothers would've got confused. But Shankar Master looked a tad older, possibly weighed down by worries.

'I am Venkatesh Rao.'

Shankar composed himself, 'What can I do for you, Sir?'

'Nothing, really. Many people in the area thought that I was you. So I came to see you on a whim.'

'Please be seated, Sir.' Shankar paused. 'I'm sorry, this is a poor man's house.'

Venkatesh sat down quietly.

'Manda, bring two cups of tea.'

'Please don't bother. I've come here only to meet you. Isn't our situation very rare? Did your parents have siblings or cousins that they lost touch with? Maybe that will explain why we look similar.'

Shankar also sat down and wiped his sweaty forehead. He said, 'Sir, my father's name is Setu Rao and my mother's name is Bhagavva. I have never seen my father. In fact, I don't even have a picture of him. He died when I was still in my mother's womb. But I know that both my parents didn't have any siblings. I am their only child. What about you, Sir?'

'I'm an only child too,' said Venkatesh. 'My father's name is Madhav Rao and my mother's name is Indiramma. We've never visited this part of Karnataka and we don't have any relatives here either.'

Both men fell silent.

'Well, that theory doesn't explain the mystery then. I am really curious about our resemblance. Tell me, have you ever been to Mysore?' asked Venkatesh.

'No, Sir, never. Our family is settled around the Ron, Navalgund and Nargund areas. I haven't crossed the Dharwad district borders even during my service. I've been working in Shishunal for ten years now and am tired of asking for a transfer to Hubli, Dharwad or Gadag.'

Mandakini interrupted their conversation as she brought tea for them in steel tumblers. 'This is Sudama's hospitality—a poor man welcoming a rich man,' Shankar said. 'Please drink some tea. We are happy that you came to our house.'

'May I meet your mother too?'

'She's in Shishunal. I work there from Monday to Saturday afternoon and then I visit my family in Hubli till Monday morning. You can visit my mother in Shishunal, or I can bring her here sometime.'

Venkatesh didn't want to inconvenience Shankar's mother. He said, 'Well, I'm planning to see Sharif's holy tomb in Shishunal. It's better that I go and visit your mother during my trip there.'

Shankar nodded. 'Where are your parents?' he asked.

'My parents and grandmother passed away within three years of each other. That was years ago.'

'I'm sorry to hear that, Sir.' He added, 'The other day, a friend came home and asked me for a bag that he'd given to me. I didn't know what he was talking about. Did he give the bag to you?'

'Yes, someone did. In fact, three or four other people also made the same mistake.' Venkatesh saw Mangalabai peeping into the room and overhearing their conversation. She seemed amazed at the resemblance too.

'OK, Shankar Master. I'll take your leave now. Goodbye, Manda, all the best to you.'

Venkatesh waved out to Mandakini and Shankar as he exited their home. He was happy that he had met them; they were such a simple family. As he walked out of the chawl, he saw people watching him. Quickly, he walked to his car and drove away.

6

Revelation

A few weeks later, the Patils were busy organizing a big moonlit dinner in their house. The rainy season had given way to clear skies and the upcoming full moon day was going to be quiet and beautiful.

'Rao ji, the dinner will be on our terrace today,' Anant Patil told Venkatesh, as they sat down to some evening snacks. 'You are not going to order home delivery or go to anyone's house for dinner. It's going to be a special night.'

'Why? What's special about tonight?'

'Sunita has a friend named Sarala. She's conducting a music programme at our house. I'm sure that you'll like it. We've only invited a few close friends.'

Vijayabai called out to her husband, 'Look here, all the dinner entrées and desserts must be white in colour tonight; the menu includes curd rice, white pudding, *kheer*, sweet white *chiroti*, rice *upma*, cabbage sabji and . . .'

By now, Venkatesh was able to understand her Hubli dialect perfectly. He had picked up the local Kannada and learnt the meanings of several colloquial terms used in Hubli.

'Enough, enough,' Patil yelled back. 'Don't dye your hair white to match the food too!'

Venkatesh laughed. Sometimes, he envied Anant Patil's life; it was full of joy and enthusiasm. Both husband and wife enjoyed each other's company and troubled each other like teenagers. It wasn't that they didn't have problems— their son was away for work in a mediocre job, they had a bedridden old mother to take care of and they had to find a groom for Sunita. Since the Patils didn't have any inherited or ancestral property, they had taken a big loan to construct the house they were now living in. But Patil wasn't anxious about it. He would reassure his wife, 'Vijaya, don't worry about it. We will repay it somehow.'

In spite of all their troubles, they had a straightforward approach to life.

But things were very different in Venkatesh's family. It was always about earning more and more money. Shanta would often take loans and then complain to her daughter, 'Gauri, I've taken a bank loan to buy that new estate in Coorg. I can't relax till it's repaid.'

'Amma, why did you take the loan if it was going to stress you out?'

'I took it because your father can get bank loans with a minimal interest rate. It's business, Gauri.'

Their family had everything, but there was no intimacy between the four of them. They lived, worked and went out together—it was mechanical. During every social event, Shanta would whine, 'Oh, I don't want to go. I really don't like the food they eat or the way they dress, but we have to. Otherwise, our hosts will think that we are rude.' But when Shanta met the hosts at the event, she would smile brightly and say, 'Heartiest congratulations on your new home. You have built a palace! And of course, you're looking stunning today!'

All their relationships were social, shallow and artificial.

Soon, Patil's guests started arriving and the hosts became busy welcoming them.

The night was cool and Venkatesh shivered. His mind turned to Shankar, 'How can we look so similar? Patil says that there are seven lookalikes all over the world. So is it a coincidence? We aren't twins, for sure. I was born at 10 a.m. in the Railway Hospital in Hyderabad. When was he born? I think I should talk to Shankar's mother, Bhagavva. Maybe she can throw some light on it.'

Sarala Bapat made an entrance and the programme began immediately. She started singing and all conversation in the room stopped.

Patil sat down next to Venkatesh and whispered, 'If you close your eyes and throw a stone around here, it will hit either a poet or a musician. All good Hindustani musicians are from here—Bhimsen Joshi, Gangubai Hangal, Mallikarjun Mansur, Basavaraj Rajguru and many others.'

Venkatesh did not know much about music but he knew that Patil was telling the truth. Shanta had learnt Carnatic music before marriage, but had soon given it up without a second thought. Gauri was only interested in rock music.

A minute later, Sarala was singing Shishunala Sharif's songs. '*How do I cross the plantain grove, sister, how? How shall I bring water?*' she cooed. '*How can we cross the river of life without a boat?*'

Venkatesh was impressed. Sharif dealt with meaningful themes in such simple language; it was his forte.

~

The next day, Venkatesh went to office and asked a colleague for directions to Shishunal. That Friday, Venkatesh decided to drive out alone to see Shankar and his mother. Since he was going to meet Bhagavva for the first time, he bought some fruits for her. The roads were dusty and his car was completely covered with grime by the time he reached Shishunal an hour and a half later. The village was next to a large lake and had fertile land with dark soil. The farmers grew sunflowers, jowar and toor dal.

Venkatesh found that despite Sharif's huge success, Shishunal remained a quiet and sleepy village. He parked the car in front of the primary school in the centre of the village. Hearing the sound, a man came out and asked him, 'Master, what are you doing here? I thought that you had taken the day off.'

'I am not Master.'

The man peered at him, 'Are you a relative?'

'Yes,' lied Venkatesh. He wanted to avoid more questions.

'So you've come to see the hill, Saheb?' the man asked.

'What hill?'

'The holy tomb of Sharif. People come from everywhere just to see it.'

'Yes, I want to visit the tomb. But first, can you direct me to Shankar Master's house?' In a small village like Shishunal, everybody knew everybody's business. Venkatesh was hopeful that this man would help him find Shankar's house.

'Look there,' the man pointed to a banyan tree. 'His house is right next to it. You're in luck; he's at home today.'

Venkatesh smiled and thanked him.

He walked over to Shankar's house and knocked at the door. There was no response. When he knocked again, a voice from inside said, 'Master will not take tuitions today.'

Venkatesh knocked once more. The same voice replied without opening the door, 'We are performing some rituals at home right now. Please come back in the evening.'

'I am Venkatesh. I've come from Hubli,' he said loudly.

'Which Venkatesh—Salimani Venkatesh or Deshpande Venkya?'

'No, I . . .' his voice trailed off. He thought, 'What should I say? That I'm the Venkatesh who resembles Shankar?' Out loud, he said, 'I'm from State Bank of India in Hubli . . .'

'Avva, whom are you talking to?' Venkatesh heard Shankar's faint voice.

'It's some person called Venkatesh from a bank in Hubli.'

'Ask him to come inside.'

'On this occasion?' she sounded surprised.

'Please, Avva, let him in.'

Finally, the door opened and Venkatesh came face-to-face with an old Brahmin widow. She appeared strong even though she was very thin. She was wearing a torn white sari with the pallu over her clean-shaven head.

'This must be Shankar's mother,' Venkatesh thought. He looked at her with mixed feelings; there was surprise and anxiety.

'Please come in and sit,' she said, and pointed to a broken chair. 'We were not opening the door because we are performing *shraddha* today.'

'Bhagavva, where's the holy grass?' interrupted the priest performing the rituals. The old woman excused herself and went inside.

Venkatesh sat down. He thought, 'Had I known it was Shankar's father's death anniversary, I wouldn't have come today. But how could I have known? Poor Shankar, he's been performing this ritual almost since he was born. It is improper for an outsider like me to be present on such an occasion.' He said loudly, 'Master, please go ahead with the shraddha. Meanwhile, I'll visit the Holy Hill and come back here.'

'Sir, I can't go out with you today, but you've come all the way from Hubli and we'd like you to eat lunch with us; it's the prasad of our forefathers. You may go visit the tomb, but please come back soon,' Shankar told him.

Venkatesh nodded and set out for his destination, still thinking about the shraddha. He knew how it was done. His father's shraddha fell on the twelfth day after Dussehra, before the festival of Diwali. On that day, the family was supposed to eat at 6 a.m. and fast thereafter. However, Shanta never performed such rituals at home. Instead, she gave five thousand rupees to the Banashankari Mutt to perform them. On the day of the shraddha, Shanta would go to the mutt, bow down before the *pinda* or the rice ball representing the dead person's soul. Then she'd eat two bites reluctantly and come back home, whereas Venkatesh would go alone at 4 a.m. and perform the ritual with sincerity. After that, Shanta wouldn't remember her father-in-law until the next year.

Venkatesh remembered his father, Madhav Rao. He hadn't lived long after his son's marriage. He had loved Shanta like his own, especially because he didn't have daughters. Madhav Rao was a gentle man who obeyed his mother while she was alive and then obeyed his daughter-in-law until the day he died. It was such a long time ago. After his paralytic attack, his father had tried to say something to him, but Venkatesh hadn't been able to understand him. It was the first time he had seen his father become angry and frustrated.

Soon, Venkatesh reached the Holy Hill. The place symbolized harmony between two communities and had devotees everywhere, irrespective of religion. People firmly believed in Sharif. The tomb was located under the shade of a neem tree. Venkatesh offered a hundred rupees at the dargah and was blessed with a broomstick of peacock feathers by the maulvi.

A man standing near him remarked, 'You look like Master, but you can't be him.'

'You're right. How did you know?'

'Because the poor Master can't afford to offer a hundred rupees. Are you related to him?'

'Yes.'

'You are not from around here. Have you come to visit him?'

Venkatesh had never experienced this in Bangalore. The people here kept asking questions and dragged the other person into a conversation even if he or she was a stranger. Venkatesh did not answer the man and simply walked away.

When he came back to Shankar's house, another acharya had joined in. Mantras of shraddha were being chanted loudly. Venkatesh sat outside in the veranda listening to them. He knew the sequence of the mantras. When his father was transferred to Varanasi, his grandmother had forced Venkatesh to join a Sanskrit school in the evenings. Slowly, he had developed a love for the language and continued to perform puja at home even today.

Gauri teased him often, 'Anna, why don't you take voluntary retirement and start performing pujas for everyone? You know that you'll love it.'

Ravi would also smile and agree, 'Yes, these days acharyas from India are much more in demand than software engineers. They make a lot more money too.'

But Shanta wouldn't have liked to be the wife of an acharya. Venkatesh almost smiled at the thought.

Suddenly, his attention went back to the chanting, 'My father, grandfather and great-grandfather are Setu Rao, Shrinivas Rao and Virupaksha Rao. My gotra is Shandilya. For the sake of pleasing the gods, I, Shankar Rao, perform this shraddha every year. May the forefathers come in the form of a cow, Shiva and the sun and accept the prasad I offer.'

The acharya started coughing. He had to repeat the

whole mantra again and Shankar repeated it after him.

'What's this?' Venkatesh wondered. 'I also say the exact same mantra! Only two names are different—my father's name and my name. I know for certain that my father did not have any brothers. It can't be a coincidence that the names of our paternal grandfather, great-grandfather and our gotra are the same! But his father's name is Setu while my father's name is Madhav. Shankar and I must be related somehow.'

Like a flash of lightning, it all became suddenly clear to him. The mantras had exposed the truth about Shankar and Venkatesh. So much resemblance between them! His father and Shankar's father must be the same person. They were brothers—they had to be! It was the only explanation.

For a moment, Venkatesh was happy at solving the mystery and finding a brother. Then the shock set in. He immediately grasped what this meant. His mother Indiramma's innocent face flashed before him and tears welled up in his eyes. He sat still for a long, long time.

After the shraddha, Shankar Master came to the veranda and saw him, 'Have you been waiting here for a long time, Sir? Please come inside and join us for lunch.'

'So Shankar does not know anything about this. I shouldn't jump to conclusions. It would be improper to say anything right now. I must verify everything thoroughly before I say anything to anyone,' thought Venkatesh.

He stood up and went inside the house. Banana leaves were spread out on the floor, serving their purpose as temporary plates for lunch. The menu featured thick rice, *rava* laddu and *urad* vada, among other entrées.

Bhagavva was sitting in a corner, wearing a white sari that had been mended too many times. She looked at Venkatesh and said, 'Sir, we are poor, but today's ritual demands these preparations. I hope you like them.'

Venkatesh felt awkward when she called him 'Sir'. He wanted to ask her many questions, but didn't know where to begin.

So he looked at Shankar instead and asked him, 'How many years have you been performing shraddha?'

'Since my thread ceremony when I was eight years old, Sir. It's been forty-seven years now,' said Shankar, between mouthfuls of food.

Venkatesh's mind raced to make sense of this information, 'Father died twenty-five years ago. That means father's shraddha was being performed even when he was alive!' He asked Shankar, 'What are your children's names, Master?'

'My mother's name is Bhagirathi, which is a name of the Ganga. So I named my daughters after rivers related to the Ganga—Mandakini, Alakananda and Sarayu. Manda is desperately searching for a job these days. Now even engineers have to be willing to work in bigger cities like Pune and Mumbai. But how can we send her alone?'

Bhagavva interrupted him, 'I've told Shankar to get her married.'

'I know it, Avva, but where will I find a suitable groom? Manda was born in mulanakshatra, Sir. I don't really believe in *nakshatras* and horoscopes, but a lot of other people do. In fact, according to my horoscope, my father should have been a very prosperous man, but he died before I was born. So how can I believe in all these things? Similarly, Manda's mulanakshatra is supposed to be inauspicious for the father. But I'm absolutely fine. Nothing bad has happened to me.'

'Isn't it possible to find a boy whose father has died already?' asked Venkatesh.

'Of course it is, but I also have to think about the dowry. My daughter is prepared to marry a less educated boy. But even they ask for at least twenty thousand rupees.'

'What about your other daughters?'

'My second daughter, Alakananda, is very intelligent. She obtained a top rank and easily got admission into the best engineering colleges of the state. However, I couldn't afford the fees and I enrolled her into a diploma course. She feels bad, but she doesn't say anything.'

'What about Sarayu?'

'Sarayu is in the tenth class. She's intelligent too and wants to become a doctor. Her teachers expect her to do very well.'

'Will you allow her to enter the medical field?'

'Sir, such things are possible only for people like you. We can't afford it. But Manda told me that she has decided not to get married. She will earn money by taking tuitions and then she can help Sarayu become a doctor.'

By now, lunch was almost over. Venkatesh had barely touched his food. He thought sadly, 'The three girls are good, but thanks to their father's poverty, they can neither be educated well nor can they be married.'

He wanted to talk to Bhagavva. He thought, 'How do I manage to talk to her without Shankar around?'

There was a sudden knock at the door. It was the school peon. He had come from the school to tell Shankar that he was needed there immediately because the headmaster was indisposed. Shankar got ready to leave—the holy sandal paste from the ceremony was still smeared on his forehead.

Venkatesh breathed a sigh of relief. He'd be able to talk to Bhagavva after all.

Shankar apologized, 'Sir, I'm sorry to leave you like this. But the headmaster will get upset if I don't go. Please relax and have some tea. I'll be back soon.'

'Don't worry, Shankar. Please take care of your responsibilities. I'll wait for you right here.'

Shankar left and Venkatesh went to the next room in search of Bhagavva. There was a faint smell of cow dung in the air. A ray of sunshine entered the room through a hole in the roof. His eyes fell upon Bhagavva who was lying on a mat; but she was not sleeping. She sat up when she saw him and offered him a mat to sit on.

He sat down and stared at her, as if he was looking at her for the very first time. 'She must have been beautiful in her youth. But now she looks burdened with poverty, widowhood and a tough life,' he thought. He asked her, 'Amma, had my mother lived, she would have been of your age today. What does Shankar call you?'

'He calls me Avva,' she said softly.

'Then I will also call you Avva. I have a question. Is Shankar related to me? Why do we look so similar?' Venkatesh asked her directly.

'I don't know. When you both sat down to eat lunch, I felt like I was looking at Shankar's brother, if he had one.'

'Tell me more, Avva. How did Shankar's father die? Maybe that will explain the mystery. As far as I know, my father didn't have any relatives in this area. Only you can help me with the story. Please, tell me what happened.'

'What do you want to know?' Bhagavva asked him gently. 'Shankar is my only child. He was born when I was sixteen years old and his father died before he could even see him. No relatives from his father's side stayed in touch or helped us. I came here and decided to make this place our home. There was nothing else that I could have done.'

'Hasn't anyone from your husband's family come to visit you? Why didn't you try to go and meet them?'

She sighed, 'It's a long story. Fifty-five years have passed.

I think I've almost forgotten what happened. I haven't told Shankar about it either. What's the use? It wouldn't have changed anything.'

'But you must tell me, Avva. Maybe it'll bring me peace. Think of me as your son.'

Bhagavva's eyes seemed to focus on something far away. He heard the clock ticking silently as she got lost in the memories of the days past. Slowly, she started narrating her story.

7

A New Life

Shurpali was a small village in Karnataka that had a temple of Narasimha and his wife Lakshmi on the banks of the river Krishna. Thousands of people attended the annual fair held here.

Bhagirathi was born in another village nearby. Her parents drowned in a flood when she was a toddler and her maternal uncle Gopal Kulkarni offered to take responsibility of the orphaned girl. He was the village postman in Shurpali. Gopal's wife, Kaveramma, scolded her frequently, 'Your parents have given you an apt name—Bhagirathi. You keep playing in the river all day!'

Gopal had a son, Hanuma, who was five years older than Bhagirathi and studied in Jamakhandi, a nearby town. Meanwhile, Bhagirathi studied up to the fourth grade. She was not allowed to study further because there was no middle or high school in the village. She didn't ask to study more either—higher education for girls was unheard of in those days and she had to help at home.

As the years passed, Bhagirathi grew up to be a very beautiful young woman. She was fair and attractive and had long, black hair. Many women were jealous of her. Kaveramma did not send her out alone often because she was afraid that someone might try to take advantage of her. Bhagirathi's only companion at home was Hanuma who was now studying in high school. Her uncle and aunt started searching for a suitable groom for her.

People asked Gopal and Kaveramma, 'Why are you searching for a groom? Your son can marry her. That'll be perfect.'

'No, Hanuma and Bhagirathi have been raised like brother and sister. It will not be a good match,' said Kaveramma.

Hanuma, Bhagirathi and Gopal also agreed with her.

The truth was that Kaveramma had completely different reasons for rejecting the match. She believed that there was no use of marrying her son to Bhagirathi because that way Hanuma would not get any dowry at all. But if he married someone else, he would get dowry and maybe other possessions too. She knew that Bhagirathi would somehow manage to get a groom.

Eventually, Kaveramma's prediction came true.

In those days, people who came to Shurpali for the

annual fair stayed with their relatives because there were no hotels in the area. That year, Champakka and her son Setu Rao came to live in Gopal's neighbour's house for a few days. The neighbour Bhima Rao had known Champakka's family from his days in Mumbai.

Champakka was also from this area, but her husband had worked in Mumbai for many years and, eventually, he had passed away there too. After that, Champakka decided to continue staying in Mumbai. She supported herself and her son Setu by working as a cook in a mutt in Matunga. Setu was now twenty-two years old and he was studying in Mumbai.

The moment Champakka laid eyes on the beautiful Bhagirathi, she wanted her son to marry her.

Kaveramma thought, 'This is the best possible match for Bhagirathi, especially since there's no demand for dowry. Moreover, this family has no close relatives or a father-in-law who will trouble her or pass sarcastic comments.'

Gopal agreed with her too.

Both the parties approved the alliance and the negotiations began. After a few days, the wedding date was set for six months later.

During this time, Setu never said anything to Bhagirathi, nor did she expect him to. He never wrote her any letters either. Every day, she sat on the banks of the river Krishna and dreamt about her future and the unfamiliar life in Mumbai. Meanwhile, Hanuma's exams were near so he sat by her side and studied while she daydreamed.

Six months passed in the blink of an eye and the marriage ceremony took place in the auspicious presence of God Narasimha. Since both the families were poor, only a few people were invited to the wedding.

After the ceremony, Setu stayed in Gopal's house for fifteen days while Champakka went to visit her relatives in other towns and villages nearby. Bhagirathi discovered that Setu was young, intelligent and very handsome. She liked him. And in turn, he loved her youth, beauty and vivacity. The two weeks passed by in a flash.

It was the end of Bhagirathi's marital bliss.

~

Tears started flowing down Bhagavva's cheeks. Venkatesh stared at her, dumbstruck.

Time stood still at a memory that was more than fifty-five years old.

~

At the end of that fortnight, Champakka laid down one condition—her son's education must be completed that year as scheduled. His studies would be disturbed if Bhagirathi came to Mumbai with him now; she must stay back. After Setu's final exams, he would find a job.

Bhagirathi should join him only after that. Gopal and Kaveramma agreed to her condition but nobody asked the newly-weds for their opinion.

The next month, Bhagirathi missed her periods. Soon after, the vomiting and the nausea started. It was confirmed; she was pregnant. The news was sent to Mumbai. There was no reply for a few weeks, but then one day Gopal received a letter at home. Champakka expressed her joy but she added that this could have waited till her son was employed.

When Bhagirathi was in the sixth month of her pregnancy, Champakka came to the village to conduct the *seemantham*, a traditional baby shower. This was usually performed in the in-laws' house. But since it wasn't possible to accommodate guests in Champakka's one-room house in Mumbai, she and her stepsister Parimala came to Gopal's house for one week.

Two days after they had arrived, Parimala went to fetch water and overheard some women gossiping. One of the women said, 'Bhagirathi is always sitting with Hanuma on the banks of the river. Kaveramma should keep an eye on her.'

'Who knows what's really going on?' added another woman who was extremely jealous of Bhagirathi and her handsome husband. 'Clever Gopal has married Bhagirathi to a boy who stays far away from here.'

'The girl is so lucky. She was so intimate with Hanuma

and yet, she's managed to find another nice boy,' the first woman commented.

'These people from Mumbai must have fallen for Bhagirathi's good looks. They didn't even bother to find out more details about her. Did you know that she pretended to get pregnant right after her marriage? Even the midwife Hakinabi says that she's seven months pregnant now. I think that she must already have been one month along at the time of her marriage.'

Parimala could not restrain herself after listening to this. She went and met Hakinabi immediately. Parimala asked her, 'I have heard so many good things about your expertise. Tell me, how is the health of our dear Bhagirathi? When do you think she'll deliver?'

Without batting an eyelid, Hakinabi answered, 'Bhagirathi is doing very well. Her foetus is big—it may be six or seven months old. By the grace of Allah, she'll give birth to a boy. I'll take care of her with all my heart. Then you must give me a good Ilkal sari.'

'Of course, why not?'

Parimala was now sure that Bhagirathi was seven months pregnant and with someone else's child. She thought that she should wait till the seemantham was over, and then she would tell her sister about her finding on their way back to Mumbai.

The seemantham went off as planned. Champakka gifted Bhagirathi a pair of her old gold earrings, a green blouse and some fruits. She blessed Bhagirathi and said, 'I pray for a safe delivery. I will come back for your son's naming ceremony.'

~

'Then she said goodbye,' whispered Bhagavva as she wiped her tears. 'We never met after that.'

'It's almost like a movie,' Venkatesh thought. He waited for her to continue.

~

As planned, Parimala accompanied Champakka on her return journey and said, 'Sister, you're so innocent. You didn't find out about Bhagirathi's character before getting your son married to her. The girl's cousin—that boy Hanuma—is very intimate with her. You had already asked the couple to wait until Setu completed his education and found a job. Have you ever thought about how she became pregnant despite your instruction? Look at her belly—it's so big and so soon! The midwife Hakinabi and the other women in the village can't stop talking about it.'

At first, Champakka didn't quite believe her, but Parimala kept poisoning her mind. Champakka was already unhappy because she was sensing that Setu was distancing himself from her after his marriage. Suddenly, this became a good explanation for the drift. By the end of the journey, Parimala had completely convinced Champakka that Bhagirathi was already pregnant when she married her son.

At home, Champakka tried to tell her son 'the truth', 'Look here, Bala, something's definitely fishy. Think, why didn't anybody in the village marry her despite her beauty? Unfortunately, you've become the unsuspecting victim of her charm. Promise me that you will leave her.'

'But Avva . . .'

'Don't. Just don't say a word. I know how the world works. She's a fallen woman and she'll deliver in the eighth month. Think about it; you'll become a father within eight months of marriage. Even you were born after the tenth month. I'm your mother and I want the best for you. I can't stay with a loose woman like her. You can stay if you want to. Parimala must have already spread the word among our relatives. I shouldn't have taken her with me.'

No matter what Setu said or did, Champakka did not change her mind. She sat down and wrote a letter to Bhagirathi's uncle.

After a few weeks, Gopal received the life-changing letter. It was a bolt from the blue. Champakka simply wrote, 'We don't want your niece. You can keep her. The baby is Hanuma's and not my son's. We will not take her back.'

Hanuma was furious, 'How can she say such things?

I am willing to swear on anyone—Bhagi is like my sister. As it is, I was worried about how she would live with that devilish mother-in-law. What is Setu doing to correct this? Can't he convince his mother that she's wrong?'

Young and pregnant Bhagirathi collapsed in grief. At last, she told Hanuma through her tears, 'Please go to Mumbai and meet my mother-in-law and husband. Fall at their feet and beg them for mercy. Tell them Bhagirathi is as pure as Sita. There's no *agnipariksha* in this Kalyug, otherwise I would've jumped into the fire and proved my chastity. Tell my husband that he's the only man I've ever been with. I want to go myself, but I can't travel in this condition and Uncle won't be able to travel to Mumbai alone because he doesn't know the local language or English.'

Hanuma put a reassuring hand on her shoulder and said, 'Don't worry; I'll go to Mumbai and bring your husband back.'

He had never been to Mumbai before, but his friend Chintamani Kale had gone there a few years ago to visit his aunt. Hanuma told Chintamani about the situation and the two of them travelled together to Mumbai.

When young Hanuma got off the train in Mumbai early in the morning, he was confused upon seeing the big city; it was much larger than Jamakhandi and Bijapur. In addition, he didn't know Hindi or Marathi. Troubled, he turned to Chintamani, 'Here's the address, but how will

I find my brother-in-law in such a large city? Maybe we should go back.'

Then Hanuma remembered Bhagi's tearful face. He said, 'No, I can't go back yet. I must find Setu first.'

It took a few hours for the two boys to locate the chawl in Matunga. When they reached Champakka's house, they found it locked.

In Marathi, a neighbour asked them whom they were looking for.

'Setu Rao or his mother, Champakka,' said Chintamani.

'Setu has a job interview in Pune. So both mother and son have gone there by train just this morning.'

'When are they back?'

The neighbour shrugged, 'I don't know. Maybe three or four days. Who are you? Why don't you leave a message for them?'

Hanuma shook his head. The message he was carrying had to be communicated in person. Disappointed, the boys went to Chintamani's aunt's house.

When they were resting in the afternoon, there was breaking news on the radio from the Dadar railway station. The Deccan Queen, which had left Mumbai that morning, had met with an accident in the ghats on its way to Pune. Several bogies had turned upside down. The listeners were advised to contact the railway police for more details.

Hanuma and Chintamani rushed to the railway station. There were so many people there—some were in shock while others were confused and weepy.

Hanuma was dumbstruck and sat down on the floor. Chintamani ran to make inquiries and came back with a sad face just minutes later. He told Hanuma that Setu and Champakka's names were on the list of the deceased.

Hanuma started crying bitterly, 'What am I going to tell Bhagi?'

Chintamani said, 'Don't give up, Hanuma. The railway staff is taking the passengers' relatives to the scene of the accident. Let's go there and confirm their identity before we think further.'

When they reached the spot, they saw that the bogies had rolled down right into the valley. Body parts were scattered everywhere. It was a ghastly sight. There was no way anyone could identify all the dead bodies. In the end, the railway department informed everyone that they were going to conduct a common cremation before the unclaimed bodies started stinking. Disheartened, the two boys returned to Jamakhandi the same night, along with a newspaper that contained the names of those who had died in the accident.

Meanwhile, Bhagirathi was waiting at home, desperately believing that Hanuma would somehow convince Setu. She had not eaten properly since the letter had come from Mumbai. Sometimes, she would get angry with the unborn baby and think, 'Isn't it because of this baby that people are talking ill of me? Maybe I should starve myself so that it will die inside my womb. But what do I do? It's a part of me and a part of Setu too. The baby is my reason to live. Had I not been pregnant, I would have drowned myself in the river Krishna days ago.'

When Hanuma returned from Mumbai, Bhagirathi was waiting for him all dressed in red like a married woman. When she heard that she had become a widow, she couldn't take it any more and fell to the floor in a faint before anyone could catch her. A short while later, she went into labour. Instantly, Hakinabi was called for. She was surprised to find that Bhagirathi had a lot of fluid in the womb, which explained the big stomach. After eighteen hours, Bhagirathi gave birth to a tiny premature baby boy.

And that's how Shankar was born. No one rejoiced or celebrated his birth—he was an unwanted child.

8

Uncovering the Past

In the old days, the Brahmins in Shurpali were very orthodox, and Bhagirathi—a teenage mother and a widow—was bound by customs and traditions. It was mandatory for her to shave her head to be considered purified, thus clearing her husband's path to heaven. Her long, shining black hair was cut and her head shaved. Bhagirathi was barely aware of what was happening to her. For a few weeks, she lived her life a day at a time.

Unfortunately, Chintamani spread the news in the entire village that Bhagirathi's husband had deserted her. It was a matter of great disgrace not only for her, but also for Hanuma and his parents. The family could not step out of their house without somebody passing comments or turning up their nose at them.

Kaveramma would openly curse her and talk about

her to everybody who came home, 'This girl has been an endless burden and a curse to our family. She killed her parents as soon as she was born, and then she killed her husband as soon as she was married.'

Bhagirathi was just beginning to accept the cruel hand that fate had dealt her, but then came the month of Shravana—the festive time of the year. It was a month of great joy for married women, who would wear new clothes and jewellery, worship Mangla Gauri and pray for their husbands' long life. It was an ill omen to see a widow on such an occasion and the entire village shunned Bhagirathi. Everybody avoided her like the plague.

One night, after she had rocked her son to sleep, she looked out of the window. At a distance, she could see the villagers celebrating with their friends and families. She thought about her future, 'I had my dreams too, just like every girl. But destiny has shattered them. There's nothing that life can offer me now. Who cares about my child or me? Nobody. Why should we live? I don't have the strength to face this harsh world day after day. Yes, it's better to put an end to such a life.'

Later that night, after the festivities were over and everyone had gone home, she held her son close and walked to the river. It was the night of the new moon. The sky was dark and her surroundings were deathly quiet. The river Krishna was full. She smiled. It was perfect. Her life flashed before her eyes. Setu had come into her life like a ray of sunshine, but he had left her alone in darkness and an unending ocean of misery.

Suddenly, Bhagirathi was not afraid. She had no desire to live, so there was nothing to fear. With the baby clinging to her bosom, she walked into the icy waters. She prayed to the river, 'I am an unfortunate orphan. Krishna, you are my mother and I'm coming to be with you forever. You know the truth about me—I am pure. Take me into your arms and rid my baby and me of this disgraceful life.'

She stepped further into the water until it came up to her waist. Just then, baby Shankar started crying. Out of nowhere, a fisherman, Chouda, came running towards the noise. He was a strong man and his eyes were red from drinking too much. As he reached the shore, he grasped the situation at once. Without a moment's delay, he jumped into the river and dragged Bhagirathi out of the water. He scolded her, 'Find a way to live with Mother Krishna's help. Don't be a fool. Why do you want to die and go against all that she stands for?'

Bhagirathi looked at her saviour and wept.

Chouda consoled her as he walked her to his hut, 'Be brave, sister, joys and sorrows are a part of life. Look, even Satya Harishchandra suffered in his life. You have a beautiful son; live for his sake. It's your duty to raise him to be a good man. God will be with you every step of the way.'

Bhagirathi decided not to stay in the village where her

life and that of her son's would be worse than a dog's. The best way was to leave the village forever and make a fresh start somewhere else.

~

The next morning, Gopal Kulkarni found Bhagirathi and her baby missing. They searched for her everywhere but she was nowhere to be found. After a few days, the villagers came to the conclusion that she had committed suicide.

Gopal and Hanuma were extremely upset and couldn't bear to live in the same house any more. They cursed Setu for ruining Bhagirathi's life. Gopal asked for a transfer and the whole family left to live in another village far away.

Meanwhile, Bhagirathi found her way to distant Dharwad. To make both ends meet, she started working in people's houses as a cooking maid, earning meagre wages.

Time passed and Shankar grew up in poverty and without a father to protect him. Bhagirathi registered the boy's name in school as Shankar Setu Rao Joshi. She kept her tragic history a secret from her son because she wanted Shankar to respect and love his dead father. Since Setu was thought to be dead, she dutifully performed his shraddha on his death anniversary every year. At times, Shankar asked her many questions about his father and where he was from. Since Bhagirathi herself didn't know for sure, she couldn't answer his questions and usually stayed silent or distracted him by asking him something else.

So the mother and the son struggled to manage by themselves, and in the process, learnt to be independent. Bhagirathi worked hard; she bathed newborns, took care of their mothers and cooked for people. In time, her hands became rough and she toughened up. A long time ago, she had been a beautiful girl. But not any more.

As Shankar grew into a young man, he felt sad to see his mother toiling in others' homes. After his school-leaving exams, he decided to discontinue his studies. As luck would have it, he found a job as a primary schoolteacher. Still, Bhagirathi continued to work to help her son.

Shankar was later transferred to different places in his job and, in due course of time, married a nice girl and had children of his own.

~

'That's how I raised Shankar,' said old Bhagavva.

Venkatesh sat there, listening in horror. He stared at her. It seemed unbelievable that she had been subjected to so much injustice, but she was living proof that this was not a story. It was her reality. He couldn't imagine the agony that lay inside her heart. Still, he wondered out loud, 'Are you certain that your husband died in the accident?'

'Son, no Indian woman would ever say that her husband

had died if he hadn't. The news of his death appeared in the papers too. I have preserved the extract. Wait here, I'll show you.'

Bhagavva stood up and went into the next room. She brought back an old torn piece of cloth, which she unwrapped, and then uncovered a newspaper cutting. The paper was yellow and discoloured with age; her husband's name had been underlined. She showed him a small envelope and took out a stamp-sized photograph of her husband.

There was no doubt—it was his father. But Venkatesh didn't understand; why did people call him Setu here?

'These are the only physical remnants of my past. When we were married, there were no photographs to capture the moment. It was expensive to do that in those days and both our families were poor. But when my husband left to go to college, he gave me this picture. Sometimes, when I can't recollect his face, I take it out and look at it. My Shankar looked exactly like him at that age.'

Venkatesh hardly heard her. He was still pondering over why his father was known by a different name. He asked Bhagavva, 'What was your husband's name?'

'Setu—that's what everybody called him. I also used that name during our marriage rituals.'

Venkatesh noticed that she didn't blame the man who had left her pregnant and alone. He probed further, 'What did Champakka call her son at home?'

Venkatesh still hoped to discover that maybe this man was not his father after all.

'Bala,' she said simply.

Yes, it was him. Venkatesh had no doubt any more.

Tears were flowing down Bhagavva's cheeks.

Knowing his father, Venkatesh was sure that he must have kept some souvenir of his old life. He asked, 'Avva, what did your family give Setu during the wedding?'

'We were really poor back then. I think Uncle Gopal gave him one hundred rupees as dowry and a ring.'

'What kind of ring?'

'A gold ring with the letter "bha" written in Sanskrit.'

'What happened to the property and your husband's other belongings after the railway accident?' asked Venkatesh.

'Who knows? My husband had deserted me. Why would my family go to Mumbai to inquire further? Maybe Parimala took away everything. We were too upset to think about it.'

She paused. Then she folded her thin bony hands, 'Son, I swear in the name of God Shiva, I have never disclosed this tale to anyone before. You were so concerned . . . maybe it was time for me to tell someone. Shankar knows that he was born after his father's death, but he doesn't know anything else. He should never find out that his father had humiliated and left me. Please, promise me that you'll never tell anyone about this.'

Venkatesh looked at her hands. These were no ordinary hands; they had toiled for a lifetime to raise a son. These hands belonged to the mother who had quietly bowed down and accepted the injustices heaped upon her by men and fate. Now she was requesting him to keep them a secret so that Shankar didn't think less of his father. How could he tell anyone? Venkatesh came forward, took Bhagavva's hands into his and touched her feet. He could feel the tears in his eyes. Silently, he apologized to her without saying the words out loud, 'Please forgive my father, if possible.'

When Shankar returned from school, Venkatesh was ready to leave and didn't wait for teatime. He drove back to Hubli with a heavy heart, 'Will Bhagavva ever forgive my father once she learns the truth?' he wondered. 'Should I even tell them what actually happened? Right now, Bhagavva and Shankar are least bothered about why we look alike. They have more important things on their minds.'

When Venkatesh reached Hubli, he found that the Patils were busy preparing for a trip to Gokarna, Murdeshwar and Karwar. They tried to persuade Venkatesh to accompany them, but he refused, 'I have to make an urgent trip to Bangalore. I will be back in a few days.'

'Why, Sir, you are talking as if it is a matter of life and death.'

'Yes, it is,' thought Venkatesh. 'It is someone's life and death. I have to set things right before it's too late.'

9

Seeking the Truth

Back in Bangalore, Shanta and Ravi were too busy to notice that Venkatesh was preoccupied. Shanta was busy acquiring a cardamom plantation near Coorg and with her plans for the new software company. What percentage of the shares should be given to Gauri and Ravi? Should Gauri get fewer shares because she would go away after she got married? Shanta was troubled by such thoughts. Meanwhile, Ravi was also engaged with his new company and the unfortunate downturn of the share market.

But the most important item on their list was the earnest search for suitable girls.

Earlier, Ravi had wanted to marry a computer engineer or an MBA, but after returning from America, he told his mother over dinner, 'Amma, I've realized that life is only about business. Think about it—parents raise their children so that they will look after them when they get old. That's emotional business. Marriage is like that too. My partner and I should know what to expect from each other, or else it will be a discordant match like that of Appa and you.'

Shanta smiled in agreement, 'Yes, Ravi. I'm glad that you have given this some consideration. What are you looking for in a girl?'

'My wife must have good social contacts and her parents should be affluent and well-known publicly.' Then he thought of Gauri and added, 'I don't want a girl who is idealistic. In today's world, it'll be hard to live with a girl like that.'

'Look, we already have a dozen proposals in hand. My father has sent the details of some IAS officers' daughters too. I have shortlisted three girls—Pinki, Ramya and Divya. Talk to each of them individually over a meal or coffee in a five-star hotel and make your decision. However, don't give any of them a commitment yet, okay?'

'Of course, Amma,' said Ravi.

Shanta was inclined towards Pinki, but she didn't tell her son that. 'It's not the right time,' she thought. 'Let me get his feedback first, but I hope he likes Pinki too. Her family is very well connected. Her father is close to the chief minister and will definitely become a partner in Ravi's company. Then we can easily get capital and ensure publicity. Her uncle also has a software company in New

York, and with his direction, Ravi's business can take off quickly.'

While the mother and son were busy planning their next course of action, Venkatesh was in the bedroom thinking about Bhagavva. Almost all the characters in her story were dead—his father Madhav Rao, grandmother Champakka, uncle Gopal Kulkarni and his wife Kaveramma. Hakinabi was probably dead too. Though Venkatesh knew that the man in both the cases was his father, he couldn't understand the mystery of Setu and Madhav. He fell into a troubled sleep.

That night, something woke him up at 1 a.m. and he sat bolt upright. He recalled that Champakka had once told him that Parimala and his father were of the same age, but that she barely met Parimala because she persistently asked for money. The first and the last time that Venkatesh had met Parimala was during his thread ceremony in Tirupathi when he was eight years old. 'Maybe she's still alive!' He was excited at the thought.

He stood up and went to the kitchen to drink some water. He wondered, 'Should I try and meet Parimala? Will she tell me the truth?'

On the way back to his bedroom, Venkatesh peeped into his daughter's room and found her studying at the desk.

Gauri saw him and asked, 'Anna, why are you awake? I can't sleep because I have exams. You're so lucky that you don't have to study.' She grinned.

When he didn't smile back, she probed, 'What happened? Why do you look so worried?'

When he didn't respond, she asked, 'Are you worried about Ravi's wedding? Please don't. Ravi and Amma think that marriage is a way of enhancing their status in society to bring in more business and money. Let them do what they want, Anna. Don't even bother.'

Venkatesh nodded and went back to his room. Gauri was left speculating what serious problem was eating her father, but she knew that he would tell her sooner or later.

The next day, after Gauri returned from college, her father asked her, 'When do your exams start?'

'They are fifteen days away.'

He paused, 'I thought I'd wait until your exams are over before talking to you, but I can't wait any more, Gauri.'

'What is it, Anna? Come, let's sit down and talk. You know you can tell me anything.'

Venkatesh told his daughter everything—from the day he had visited the jeweller's shop in Shiggaon to the day Bhagavva had folded her hands in front of him. Gauri saw the shock and confusion in her father's eyes. Unconsciously, she held his hand. He continued, 'Child, I can't stop thinking about my father. He was a puppet in the hands of his stubborn mother. She had struggled hard to raise him, but she monopolized his life and his feelings. Poor Bhagavva! Champakka ruined her life and her son's life too. Gauri, you're going to be a doctor. Tell me this—how can a really big pregnant woman deliver after eight months of marriage? Would you say that she became pregnant before her wedding?'

Gauri sighed, 'No, Anna, I wouldn't jump to that conclusion. A pregnant woman's stomach may be big for a variety of reasons such as too much water and a small baby, or a large baby, a tumour, or something else. Now, we can scan and explain everything. Bhagavva could have delivered early because of the shock too.'

'Weren't she and her son subjected to a great injustice?'

'Of course they were. This has been going on since the ancient times. It's always a goat that is victimized and not a tiger. A woman is usually meek and humble and that's why Bhagavva suffered the way she did. Do you know that if a retarded baby was born in Europe, people would say that the woman had delivered Satan? They'd throw stones at her and eventually kill her. If a fair child were born to dark parents, people suspected the mother of infidelity. Even now, there are people who burn their wives and daughters-in-law alive for bearing a female child. Though it is the man's chromosomes that decide the baby's gender, it's the woman who's punished.'

Venkatesh was sad, 'My father had once told me that he was supposed to travel by a certain train, but he missed it. That train met with an accident later and he considered his life after that to be a rebirth and a second chance for him. But Bhagavva shaved her head and lived like a widow from the age of sixteen until now.'

Gauri was curious, 'But Anna, how did their names come in the newspaper?'

'It was a mistake due to all the chaos. Grandma Champakka and my father weren't even on the train and the railway office got it wrong. Then Father got through the railway department exams and his transfers were in distant places like Delhi and Jammu. It must have been a good reason for both mother and son to get away from this whole episode. Later, Grandma got Father married to my gentle mother from distant Gundlupet, a village near Ooty. My mother must have had a horrible time with her ferocious mother-in-law. And yet, she was luckier than Bhagavva.'

'I agree, Anna,' Gauri said.

'I'm sure that my mother didn't know anything about her husband's first marriage. I think that's why Grandma Champakka didn't allow us to get close to any relatives. We all remained unaware of my father's past.'

'Leave it, Anna. What happened is in the past now. Tell me, how can I help you? What do you want to do?'

'I've thought about it. I want to go to my father's locker in the State Bank of India tomorrow, but your mother keeps all the locker keys and I can't just ask her. I haven't opened the locker in years and she'll ask me a hundred questions.'

After Madhav Rao's death, the locker was held in Venkatesh's and Gauri's names jointly since it contained

Venkatesh's parents' jewellery and gold. Shanta had lockers in other banks, and didn't really care for the contents of this locker. Gauri replied, 'Relax, Anna. I understand. This is not the time to tell Amma about Bhagavva. I'll get the key from her.'

Both mother and daughter often discussed Gauri's lack of fascination for jewellery. She preferred to wear two thin gold bangles and small stud earrings. Shanta would scold her, 'You must wear more gold. What will people think about us?'

Gauri didn't argue with her mother, nor did she get angry.

When she asked for the locker key from her mother the next evening, Shanta was very happy thinking that Gauri was finally getting interested in jewellery; but she still inquired, 'Why do you want to go to the locker? There are enough ornaments at home for you to choose from.'

'Amma, your jewellery is very heavy for my taste. I want to wear something light for Ravi's engagement. Since I have some time before my exams start, I want to check if there's something suitable for me in the locker.'

'Well, I don't think you'll fancy anything there. Those ornaments belonged to your great-grandmother. You won't like them—they're quite old and unfashionable.'

'But I like vintage jewellery,' insisted Gauri.

Shanta did not believe her, but just then, she heard Ravi's and Pinki's voices coming in through the main door of the house. She quickly gave the key to Gauri.

Gauri ran to her father, 'Oh, here's the key. We can go to the bank tomorrow.'

Absent-mindedly, Venkatesh took the key from her.

'What do you want from the locker, Anna?'

'Bhagavva's family gifted Father a ring with the Sanskrit letter "bha"; it's the only proof of their marriage. I want to see if it's in the locker.'

'Are you crazy? Don't you think your grandmother would have thrown it away? Even if it did exist, Amma must have melted it along with other old jewellery and got something else made. I don't think that the ring will be in the locker.'

'We'll find out tomorrow, Gauri.'

That night, neither father nor daughter could sleep well.

In the morning, Shanta said to Venkatesh, 'I have to go to a meeting right now but I want to speak to you about something. Let's talk soon.'

'Yes, there's something I want to share with you too.'

An hour later, Venkatesh and Gauri went to the bank in Basavanagudi. When they opened the locker, they found numerous necklaces, anklets, armlets, rings and earrings. It was a wonder that Shanta had never touched them. She had enough money to buy new ones, anyway.

'Why did Mother never use any of this?' Venkatesh wondered. He remembered his mother wearing only four thin gold bangles and a black-beaded *mangalsutra*.

'Perhaps Grandma didn't allow her to. I've never seen these at home.'

He made a thorough search of the locker's contents but could not trace the ring. He was disappointed. 'You were right, Gauri,' he said, 'that ring is not here. Let's close the locker.'

Gauri stopped him, 'Wait, Anna!' She chose a traditional gold necklace and said, 'I have to take something from the locker, or else Amma will get suspicious.'

She was right. Gauri said, 'Let's go home, Anna. I'm getting late for college.'

Venkatesh went home in low spirits. He remembered his father and his room in their old house in Basavanagudi. There was a big wooden box in that room. 'Appa used to keep it locked all the time. Nobody was allowed to touch it. Maybe the ring is in that box. Where's that box now?' he wondered.

After a few minutes, Venkatesh decided to search the attic. He climbed up there and found Ravi's old cradle, an old brass coffee filter, Champakka's grinding stone, a brass statue of Lord Shiva—and finally, he saw the brown wooden box tucked away in a corner. He was thrilled. Immediately, he opened the box—and started sneezing. The dust had triggered his allergies. After the bout of sneezing had subsided, he looked into the box again. He found an official-looking document and some religious booklets; the papers had yellowed with age and become brittle.

That's when he saw it—a small brown pouch. Carefully, he opened it and saw the glint of a gold ring. As he pulled the ring out, he saw the letter 'bha' engraved on it—exactly like Bhagavva had told him.

Venkatesh had found his proof—Madhav Rao had concealed his love for his first wife from his mother. Inside the pouch, Venkatesh found a letter and a money order form addressed to 'Bhagirathi, c/o Gopal Kulkarni, Shurpali, Taluka Jamakhandi, District Bijapur, Karnataka'. The money order had been returned because the addressee was not found. Venkatesh recognized his father's handwriting in the letter:

Forgive me, Bhagi. I don't believe my mother's accusations. Please have patience. I will come and get you when I find a job. Meanwhile, take care of your health. I am sending you this money that I saved from my scholarship, but don't tell anyone. When you get this, write to me immediately at my college address. I will write more in detail the next time.

Yours, Setu

So his father had tried to contact Bhagavva without his mother's knowledge. But the money order never reached her because she had already left Shurpali, and they never met again.

Venkatesh's eyes fell upon the old document in the

wooden box. He opened it and read the contents. It was a legal document confirming a change of name from Setumadhav Rao to Madhav Rao.

Venkatesh felt sad, 'Had Appa been able to speak during the last days of his life instead of being paralysed, maybe he would have told me his secret. Now I understand why he changed his name. Setu had died along with Bhagirathi.'

When Gauri came home from college that evening, she saw her father walking around with an old brown pouch. 'What is that, Anna?' she asked.

He handed the pouch to her and watched her open it. She held the ring in her hand and stared at the evidence in front of her.

'Gauri, I wish my father had talked to me the way I do with you. But those were the old days; it was bad manners to speak freely with your elders.'

She nodded and smiled. She loved the time they spent together.

Venkatesh added, 'I think it's time for me to meet my grandmother's stepsister Parimala. I've found her address in one of Mother's old diaries. If she is alive and well, I hope that she'll be able to tell me more. I'll go back to Hubli immediately to get this sorted out and then I'll speak to Shanta about this after my visit to Parimala.'

Gauri felt sorry, and proud of her father. He was struggling to somehow compensate for the wrong that his father had done decades ago, despite the fact that he was not responsible for Bhagavva's plight in any way. If it were anyone else in his shoes, they would not have bothered to shoulder the responsibility.

10

A Meeting with the Past

After reaching Hubli, Venkatesh wrote to Parimala at her Asundi chawl address in Mumbai and asked if he could meet her.

Within a week, he got a reply from her son Neelakantha Rao, 'My mother and I do not live in Mumbai any more. We got your message from my elder son who stays in Asundi chawl. We reside in Godbole Mala in Bijapur. My mother is too old to travel, but she'll be happy to meet you if you can come and visit her here. She stays at home all day, so you can come at any time and day convenient for you.'

That same night, Venkatesh asked Anant Patil about the bus schedule and its timings for Bijapur. Patil responded with enthusiasm, 'Rao ji, there is an early morning bus to Bijapur. In fact, why don't you take a week off and go there? My aunt's younger brother has a big pomegranate farm and he can arrange your stay too. Would you like me to accompany you? I know the city very well and can take you to Gol Gumbaz and other monuments and temples.'

Venkatesh did not want Patil to go with him since this was a delicate family matter. He replied, 'I'm sorry, Patil ji. I'm going only for work and will be back in a day.'

~

Early morning the next day, Venkatesh caught the bus to Bijapur. The bus ride was on a straight and levelled road. He passed by fields of sugar cane, cotton, wheat and many fruit orchards, but was unmindful of the scenery. After a few hours, the bus reached its destination. Venkatesh got off and suddenly became aware of his aching back. He checked into a local hotel, had a shower and ate breakfast. Then he bought some fruits and flowers and headed to Godbole Mala.

He found Parimala's home easily. When the door to her house opened, he found himself facing a grey-haired old man who greeted him, 'Namaskar, I am Neelakantha Rao. Please come inside. You are welcome to our humble abode.'

Venkatesh introduced himself.

Neelakantha wondered, 'This man is my aunt's grandson from Bangalore. Whenever Mother asked her stepsister for help, she never bothered to reply. There has been no correspondence with us all these years. Now her son has come to see us, perhaps on a goodwill visit. What's the use now?'

Still, he seated Venkatesh on an old sofa and asked, 'What will you like to drink, Sir? Something cold or hot?'

'Nothing, but thank you.'

Neelakantha introduced him to a young man, 'Sir, this is my younger son, Vinayak; he's in the final year of college in BCom.' Vinayak touched Venkatesh's feet.

Somebody called out from inside one of the rooms. Neelakantha led the way. When Venkatesh walked into the room, he saw a woman in her eighties sitting against a wall. She saw him and immediately said, 'You are Champakka's grandson, aren't you? Then you are my grandson too. Champakka always kept a distance from us, but . . .'

Neelakantha stopped her, 'Please don't dig up the past, Avva.' Then he turned to Venkatesh, 'Sir, please sit down. Avva is old now. Don't take anything she says personally.'

The old woman was quiet after that initial outburst. Venkatesh asked Neelakantha, 'Where do you work?'

'I served in the state transport department; I am retired now.'

Parimala said, 'Neelakantha has four children—two girls and two boys. The two daughters are married while the eldest boy lives in Mumbai. The rest of us stay here in Bijapur with Vinayak.'

Neelakantha's wife Parvatibai called him aside and whispered rather loudly for Venkatesh to hear, 'We have a marriage to attend and we're getting late. Are you coming or not? If not, I have to go anyway. If this man is your relative, I'll give him something to eat before I leave. Just look at him; he's not brought anything even though he's visiting us for the first time.'

Venkatesh understood. He told his hosts, 'I'd like to stay here for some time. I have eaten my lunch already. Please go ahead with your plans. I will be fine here.'

Neelakantha replied, 'We've arranged this marriage and that's why we cannot miss it, but we'll be back in no time at all. Please feel free to stay as long as you like. In fact, you must have dinner with us tonight.'

Venkatesh nodded. He was happy to be left alone with Parimala. The moment Neelakantha and his wife left, he took out the fruits and flowers from his bag, kept them in front of the old woman and folded his hands, 'Grandmother, you are the oldest surviving member of our family. You alone know the past. Please, tell me the truth.'

Parimala was surprised, 'What is it?'

'It's about my father Madhav Rao's first marriage . . .'

'Oh yes! That was the reason that my sister Champakka and I became distant. Why do you want to bring it up now?'

'Do you remember his first wife's name?' Venkatesh asked, without answering her question.

'I think it was Bhagirathi or something like that. I met her just once.'

'Why didn't you see her again? What happened?'

Parimala took a long breath, 'People in her village said that she was pregnant before she married your father. The midwife also said so after seeing her big stomach. I told Champakka about it and she decided to desert the girl and get your father remarried. Your poor father was heartbroken at her decision.'

'Why, Grandma?'

'You must know that your grandmother was an aggressive woman. She made the decision and sent a letter to Bhagirathi's family without even discussing it with her son. After that, when your father learnt about what she had done and came to me to find out what had happened, I told him what I had heard in the village during my visit there with Champakka. He swore that Bhagirathi was as sacred as the river Ganga. He wrote to her and waited for a few weeks for a response. When there was no news, he went to the village in search of her, but she was nowhere to be found. My husband also went to help your father find his wife. Some people told them that she had committed suicide by drowning in the river Krishna with her child and her family had moved away after that incident.'

'How do you know all this?' he asked her.

'Your father told me. Perhaps she really did drown herself, but it destroyed my relationship with Champakka.'

Venkatesh was confused, 'I don't understand.'

'Your father became depressed after this incident and it took some time for him to get back to normal. Champakka blamed my husband and me because we had told your father everything. She was so furious at us for helping him that she cut off all communication with us.'

Venkatesh felt miserable. Fifty years ago, someone in the village gave his father incorrect information. As a result, poor Bhagavva lived like a widow though her husband was alive, and Madhav Rao became a widower while his wife was alive too.

He sighed and glanced at his watch. It was 2 p.m.

Parimala added, 'Later, your father agreed to get remarried for the sake of his mother. This was a long time ago. But tell me, why are you so curious?'

'Just like that.'

'Look here, son. I'm going to be direct with you. My husband helped your father a lot when he was searching for his wife. Now, I am old and maybe it's time for you to repay us. Can you give me ten thousand rupees and get Vinayak a job at your bank in Bangalore?'

Venkatesh was disillusioned. This old woman with one foot in the grave thought that his indebtedness was worth ten thousand rupees and a job. He thought of Bhagavva who was just a few years younger than Parimala. Despite her suffering and poverty, she hadn't asked him for anything. Venkatesh did not feel like folding his hands in front of Parimala after her demand. He said, 'I don't have much money with me right now. Please take this.'

He gave her one thousand rupees and walked out of the house. That evening, he caught the bus back to Hubli.

~

The next morning, Venkatesh boarded the train to Bangalore. When he reached home, his daughter greeted him. 'I'm so glad you're back, Anna. Did you have a successful trip?'

He nodded. All the pieces of the puzzle were now in place. 'I've verified everything. I'll tell your mother tonight.'

'Why did your father leave Bhagavva, Anna?'

'Gauri, my father did a great injustice to Shankar and her. Maybe it was because he was helpless, or maybe it was nobody's fault, but either way, Bhagavva suffered her entire life. Isn't it my duty to help her in any way that I can?'

'I understand that, but if you offer help out of the blue, Shankar Master will suspect your intentions and question you.'

'I know. I want to tell him the truth.'

Gauri said, 'What will you tell him—that you are the son of his father's second wife? Have you forgotten your promise to Bhagavva, Anna? What will you do if he gets angry with your father?'

'I'll tell him how Father tried to contact his mother.

I'll convince both of them that it was all a tragic misunderstanding. I'll even try to give them the money that they should have received when Appa died.'

'But what if they ask for more?' she persisted.

'I know what you're thinking. Bhagavva won't ask me for anything, I'm sure. I'll tell Shankar that I'm doing this for Bhagavva and my father. If I give their family half of what Appa left for me, he can get nothing more even through legal means.'

'Amma will say that this is foolish.'

Venkatesh sighed, 'I know that this is not the wise approach. But sometimes, we need to be unwise and still do what's right, Gauri.'

'All the best, Anna, but be prepared for the storm.'

That night, the family gathered at the dining table for dinner. Shanta ordered the cooks to lay the table and leave. She wanted to discuss family matters and didn't want the household help to overhear. She began with a question to her husband, 'Haven't you finished your work in Hubli yet? Who's going to take responsibility for Ravi's new company and his wedding?'

'Ravi's opinion is paramount for his marriage. And when it comes to planning and investing, you really know what's best for the company.'

Shanta pretended to be annoyed, 'You just thrust everything on me. Anyway, it doesn't matter. Ravi needs investors for his new company.'

'Yes, we will need at least one crore,' Ravi said. 'Of course, my partners will also pay their share. These days everything has to look exclusive and glamorous to attract global clients.'

Venkatesh turned to Shanta, 'I don't know anything about running a software company. The two of you can do as you see fit.'

'Actually, I don't have ready cash,' Shanta replied. 'I paid a lot for the cardamom estate in Coorg recently. Since the stock market is on an all-time low these days, we can't sell shares now. But I have an idea—we have rented out both the Ganga and Tunga complexes. What do you think about vacating one of them and using it for Ravi's company?'

'But then our rent will be halved.'

'So what? At least, we won't have to invest initially.' Shanta continued, 'We have other expenses coming up, too. Ravi and Pinki like each other and would like to get married soon. We have to sponsor their engagement, while Pinki's parents will take care of the wedding. We must spend at least fifteen lakhs considering our status. All these worries haunt me in my sleep.'

Poor Shanta! She couldn't sleep despite her wealth.

'But why do we need to spend fifteen lakhs for an engagement?' Venkatesh wondered out loud.

'We have to consider Veena's status and ours too. We must buy Pinki expensive gold sets. Moreover, the engagement must be in a five-star hotel where we will gift silver items to all guests and arrange a big dinner spread for them. It's going to be a lot of expenditure.'

'Not necessarily, Shanta! Grandma's gold is still there in the bank. Neither Gauri nor you have ever worn any of it. Why not give it to Pinki? We can also set up a shamiana in front of our house instead of paying a hotel. Don't treat the engagement like a business deal. We don't have to spend money lavishly.'

Shanta was livid, 'If Veena learns about your plans, she'll refuse to give her daughter to us. You'll never understand what it means to build relationships and run a business. What do you know? You've been sitting in Hubli all along!'

'Actually, I've been doing something different there. I have learnt so much about my father in the last month.'

There was something in Venkatesh's voice that made Shanta and Ravi sit up and take notice.

Venkatesh started at the beginning, and as the story unfolded, both mother and son stared at him in absolute disbelief.

II

A Father's Debt

By the end of the narration, neither Venkatesh nor Gauri could hold back their tears.

However, there was a smirk on Ravi's face. 'Well, I'm impressed,' he said. 'Though our grandfather had two wives, they didn't know about each other. He was a smart old man, wasn't he?'

Shanta asked her husband with her customary cold caution, 'What do you want to do about it?'

'I haven't yet told Shankar and Bhagavva about my findings, but I know that they live in extreme poverty and I want to help them. That's the least I can do.'

'How much?' she asked.

'Fifty lakhs. They can buy a house with ten or fifteen lakhs and they can use the rest for their children's education and marriage, or Bhagavva's medical treatment.'

Shanta and Ravi exclaimed in unison, 'Fifty lakhs!'

'I inherited two sites from my father after his death—the Ganga–Tunga complexes. Besides that, he left me gold in the bank and several fixed deposits. Today, Bhagavva and her family are in a really miserable condition and I should give them what was due to them at the time of Father's death.'

'But we're not responsible for their situation,' Shanta said angrily.

'You are right; we are not responsible at all, but when I inherited my father's property, I also inherited his share of mistakes. Appa failed in his duty towards them. We can't undo the past, but maybe we can make their lives a little easier, especially since we have so much wealth. There's no legal proof of their wedding, there's only a newspaper cutting of the accident and Appa's picture; but there is a divine court of law above us where our souls are the witnesses.'

'Stop talking about God and our souls, Dad. Let's be practical. We can't give them anything right now,' Ravi said.

Venkatesh said, 'Why not? Haven't I toiled for this home too? Thanks to your mother and her investments made from the Ganga–Tunga rent we received initially, we've earned so much more in the last twenty years. Don't forget that the start-up capital came from my father.'

'Relax, Dad. Don't get emotional. Didn't you hear what

Amma said? At the moment, we have financial problems of our own and yet, you are willing to give away fifty lakhs to someone for the sole reason that he resembles you. We all know that Grandfather was afraid of his mother. Maybe he had an affair and the old woman is simply making up a story. Why should we bother about her or her child when our grandfather himself deserted her? I feel like laughing at you. You may give him twenty thousand and close the issue.'

Venkatesh knew that his son was clever, but he hadn't known that he was heartless too. Ravi felt no compassion or empathy. What kind of a man would his son be in the future?

For the first time during the discussion, Gauri spoke. She said, 'Anna, I think you are right.'

Venkatesh turned to both his children and asked, 'What'll you do if I give away either the Ganga or Tunga complex to Bhagavva?'

Ravi replied calmly, 'I'll go to the court. That's our ancestral property and you don't have the right to just give it away without our consent. You can only donate money or property that you have earned on your own.'

Venkatesh was disheartened; his son was prepared to go to court against him and put the family honour at stake for fifty lakh rupees. How could two children raised by the same parents and in the same environment be so unlike each other, he wondered.

Shanta didn't say anything, but Gauri rushed to her father's rescue, 'Ravi, what about our family reputation? Besides, stop for a minute and think about it: Anna is right. Let him give fifty lakhs to Bhagavva who has suffered her whole life only because she was unfortunate enough to get married to our grandfather. Imagine her agony!'

Ravi turned his anger towards Gauri, 'It's very easy to advise others. Will you give away your share of the property just like that?'

'Without a second thought,' pat came her reply. 'Anna is not asking anything for himself; he's trying to compensate for the wrong done by his elders. If you want, I'll give fifty lakhs from my share of the inheritance. Anna's happiness is more important to me.'

'Do you know the value of fifty lakhs?' Ravi snapped at her. 'I'll tell you. It is a well-furnished four-bedroom house in JP Nagar, or a decent-sized site at Koramangala, or enough capital to start a new software company. If you put fifty lakhs in a fixed deposit, you'll get an income of forty thousand every month! And you want to join your father in giving that kind of money away to some old woman! It's foolishness.'

Without waiting for a reply, Ravi glared at Venkatesh and stomped out of the room.

Shanta stood up, 'Look, our son is right. If you give them fifty lakhs now, they may ask you for more later. It's better not to give them anything at all in the first place.'

'No, Shanta, trust me,' Venkatesh said. 'Shankar is not that kind of a man. Come with me and meet the family once. Then you'll understand what I'm talking about.'

She shook her head, 'It doesn't matter whether I meet them or not. I refuse to give them anything. But if you want to give them something, please give them whatever you want out of your own savings. I don't mind that at all. Goodnight.'

She too walked out of the room.

Father and daughter were left alone at the dining table. The food had become cold. Gauri put her hand on her father's shoulder in an effort to comfort him, 'Anna, don't get upset. I knew how they'd react.'

'Gauri, I was going through some old photo albums before dinner. I saw pictures of my marriage, my birthdays and my thread ceremony; everything was celebrated with so much pomp. I couldn't help thinking of Shankar who is only a few years older than me. He was completely deprived of a father and a carefree childhood. I feel bad.'

'It's getting late. Please try and sleep now. We'll figure out something in the morning.'

Venkatesh said, 'For the first time in my life, I feel horrible about not earning more money than I did. Your mother indirectly hinted that I earn less than her. The rent from the Ganga–Tunga complexes was credited to my account, but years ago, I made it a joint account with her and now she uses it for all her investments and businesses.

Today, she told me to use my personal savings when she knows very well that my only other account is my salary account, which doesn't have a fat bank balance. I spend most of what I earn on charity. There's only five lakhs there.'

'It's okay, Anna.'

'How is it okay? Both mother and son will surely take out all the money from the joint account.'

'The banks are closed at night. Come, let's go to sleep and deal with this tomorrow.'

Gauri held his hand and dragged him to the bedroom. Venkatesh was reluctant to sleep there. Today, he felt that his wife was the ugliest woman in the world. Finally, he went to the guest room, but sleep was far, far away.

Shanta was awake in the bedroom too. She knew that her husband had gone to another room to sleep, but she didn't care. She fumed, 'An old woman in a village somewhere tells him a story and he believes that she's his father's first wife. Even worse, he wants to give her fifty lakhs. He's so gullible! It's easy to give away your wife's earnings. He should first try to save some money himself.'

Shanta was also annoyed with Gauri, 'She always takes her father's side. Our family is divided into two obvious factions. I'll contact our lawyer tomorrow and make my will.'

In his bedroom, Ravi too was spending a sleepless night. 'Men are usually practical. It's my misfortune to have a father like Anna. Instead of helping me with my career, he puts obstacles in my way, and my foolish sister agrees with him. This world is about the survival of the fittest. Sometimes, we are compelled to use others as ladders to success. Anna is stupid to even think of giving away money like this,' he thought.

~

The next day, Venkatesh received a call from the head office during his morning walk. He had been transferred back to Bangalore. But he was not happy.

When he came back home, Shanta and Ravi ignored him. They didn't want to talk to him. Gauri called out, 'Anna, come here. I'm upstairs. There's a phone call for you.'

When he went up, he found that there was no phone call for him. Gauri motioned for him to peep out of the window and he saw both mother and son heading out to work. He asked, 'Gauri, why did you lie about the phone call?'

She smiled, 'Because sometimes lies beautify our lives.' She added, 'Here, Anna, take this.'

She handed him an envelope. When he opened it, he was surprised to find a cheque for forty-five lakhs in Shankar Master's name. He was speechless.

Gauri laughed at his expression, 'Amma had invested

in a fixed deposit of one crore rupees in my name to avoid income tax, or maybe it was for my marriage. Yesterday, when Ravi asked if I would give money from my share of inheritance, I thought about it again at night and realized that I don't mind it at all! I don't want someone to marry me for the sake of a crore or a nursing home. I want a boy who wants to marry me because he likes me. I want a smart boy, of course, but not someone like Ravi. Otherwise, my life will also be like yours.'

Venkatesh was proud of her. His daughter was much wiser than he had ever been at that age. He asked her, 'Gauri, your mother will find out about this. You know that. What will you do then?'

'I haven't stolen this money, Anna, nor have I given it away to a cause that I don't believe in. I'm not afraid of her or anyone else. No matter what people say, I'll always follow my conscience. It doesn't change with rank or money and it doesn't fade like fame or beauty. You have taught me that.'

Oh, his little Gauri could even talk about philosophy!

She continued, 'Anna, you can take the five lakhs out of your account and give them a total of fifty lakhs.'

'Why did you do this, Gauri?'

'That's so easy, Anna. You want to pay back a debt that your father owes somebody. I want to pay back a debt that my father owes too.'

Tears rolled down his cheeks and fell on his daughter's

hands. She didn't wipe them, but smiled and leaned against her father. It felt like a burden of generations had been lifted off their shoulders.

Mukesh

I

The Fall

It was mid-March and almost the end of the skiing season in Lausanne. Mukesh was not a stranger to this beautiful Swiss city that boasted a panoramic view of the Alps on one side and of Lake Geneva on the other. When he was younger, he had accompanied his father on business trips to Switzerland many times. While Appa was busy with his meetings, Mukesh would explore his surroundings. During one of his visits, he had learnt to ski and enjoyed the sport from then onwards, but never really became good at it.

Today, he was sitting on the deck of a resort, drinking hot coffee and feeling too lazy to ski. He admired the Alps and the reflection of the sun's rays on the snow-covered peaks. The mountains looked silver. He heard the squealing of young children next to the deck and peeked sideways to find six kids playing in the snow, trying unsuccessfully to build a snowman.

'This is such a contrast from Bangalore,' he thought to himself.

His mind wandered to his father, Krishna Rao—a self-made and soft-spoken gentleman, known as Rao Saheb to others. He had come from humble beginnings and had worked hard to become who he was today. Rao Saheb owned a huge garment export house called Mukesh Exports in Bangalore. Though he was not very highly educated, he knew every aspect of the business like the back of his hand.

Mukesh's parents had wanted him to join the family business, but he did not. They were surprised when he had studied history, language and art and had become a programme executive at BBC in London, where he was responsible for covering India's culture and heritage section. Nobody in the family had ever majored in history before. After Mukesh's employment in London, his older sister Neeraja and her husband Satish, a litigation lawyer in Bangalore, had helped Rao Saheb with the export business.

'Hey, look at me!' Mukesh heard a faint and familiar voice. He glanced around and saw Vasanthi waving at him from a short distance away.

Mukesh smiled and waved back at her.

She was wearing appropriate winter gear along with a pink headband, ski goggles, pink gloves and a pink jacket.

She was so good at skiing that nobody would ever guess that she'd grown up in Mysore in a conservative family that discouraged girls from participating in sports.

He wondered, 'Is she really the same woman that I got married to?'

Fondly, he recalled the first time that he had met her. He had come to India on a holiday to meet his family and a friend had invited him to Mysore to judge a painting competition. Vasanthi was one of the participants there.

When Mukesh had seen her for the first time, he had not been able to take his eyes off her. She was slim, fair, tall, and had long, straight hair that fell to her waist. It had been love at first sight. She was the girl he was going to marry! Amidst all his feelings, he had simply forgotten to see or judge her painting.

During the two days of his short stay in Mysore, he had gathered information about her. He had learnt that she was the youngest daughter of a pandit and had three older sisters. The family was orthodox and lived on a meagre income.

Mukesh had come back and told his family about Vasanthi. His father had agreed immediately without even seeing the girl. His mother, Sumati, had raised her eyebrows and had given him a naughty smile, 'Now I know that my Munna has grown up.' His older sister, Neeraja, had asked him to think about it and take it slow. She had been worried about the vast economic difference between the families.

Her husband, Satish, had remarked, 'When girls from poor families get married into rich ones, their attitude changes. With this girl's background, she may siphon money off quietly or buy things for her parents' home.'

Mukesh had interjected, 'She doesn't even know that I like her! I'm ready to get married to her but that doesn't mean that she wants the same thing.'

Rao Saheb had declared, 'Let's go with the proposal to the girl's parents and then we'll see what happens.'

Accordingly, Vasanthi's family had been informed. As it turned out, they happened to be from the same community as Mukesh's family. When her father had asked for Mukesh's horoscope, Rao Saheb had said, 'We don't believe in horoscopes at all. My daughter got married without any sort of horoscope-matching. If you think that the boy and our family is good, we can proceed with the wedding.'

The poor pandit had not been able to say anything more. He had known that it was the best thing that could have happened to his daughter. Mukesh was from a wealthy and respectable family that owned a huge bungalow in Sadashivnagar. The family also had a big farmhouse and a business. But more than anything else, the pandit knew that Mukesh was madly in love with his daughter.

A few months later, Vasanthi and Mukesh had been married in Bangalore; Rao Saheb had taken care of all the expenses. Sumati's happiness had known no bounds.

The day after the wedding, she had told Vasanthi, 'My child, you are just like Neeraja to me. This is your house now.' Sumati considered Vasanthi to be her daughter and Neeraja treated her like a real sister.

Soon after the wedding, the couple had moved to London and had enjoyed exploring the city together. Within a few months, Vasanthi had learnt swimming and driving. At first, she had been scared of the water and the London traffic but Mukesh had encouraged her to persist and try something new. Vasanthi had begun appreciating the differences in culture and had even cut her long hair, sporting a bob instead. The Kanjeevaram saris had been discarded and she had started wearing jeans. She had started experimenting with microwave-cooking and had begun Western classical music lessons.

Despite all these changes, Vasanthi always spoke Kannada at home. Her love for the language and the religious rituals was never in question. She had converted their storeroom into a puja room and prayed every day, just like she used to do in Mysore. Dutifully, she wore a traditional sari and sincerely performed Gauri Puja, Ganesh Puja and Lakshmi Puja every year.

Vasanthi's voice startled him, 'Whom are you dreaming of?'

Mukesh turned to her and said naughtily, 'When you're in front of me, how can I dream of anyone else? Tell me, are you ready to leave?'

'Ten more minutes, and then we'll go, all right? This is the last of the season and we won't be back until next year.'

Mukesh nodded reluctantly as she skied away from him. His eyes followed her to the top of the nearest hill and hit the blue sky. Blue was his favourite colour. His first gift to Vasanthi had been a blue sari. Unfortunately, Vasanthi hated blue and could not tell him that since it was his first gift to her. Subsequently, when he started giving her blue saris every time, she had told him, 'Mukesh, I don't like blue. It reminds me of my school uniform and the discipline and strict regime that came with it. But I love pink. It is so soft and light and full of love.' Mukesh was an artist. He had quickly understood the feelings behind the request and moved to pink saris.

From a distance, Mukesh saw Vasanthi coming down the hill. He could see her more and more clearly now. For a moment, he suddenly felt that she was skiing at a very high speed and might trip over. He forgot where he was and screamed in Kannada, 'Vasanthi, be careful! Slow down!'

People stared at him, but he did not care. His eyes were locked on his wife's figure.

He was right. Vasanthi crashed against a pine tree and fell. She screamed with pain. Two ski instructors immediately rushed to her and brought her down the rest of the hill. Mukesh ran to be by her side. Her face was red and her beautiful eyes were filled with tears—like hot water had just been splashed on a pink rose. The manager of the ski resort came at once and advised him, 'We'll give first aid but please go to the hospital right after that.'

Mukesh concurred and phoned a cab to take them to the nearest hospital. At first, he thought that the injury may be a simple muscle pull or a sprain, but Vasanthi was unable to stand or walk on her own. At the hospital, the doctor ran a few tests and finally told Vasanthi, 'I'm sorry but you have a fracture that needs immediate surgery.'

Vasanthi started sobbing. If it had been London, things would have been easier for them as they knew the doctors there and had friends who could help them. They did not know anyone here. Still, Mukesh did not want to delay his wife's medical treatment. He said, 'Let's go ahead with the surgery, Doc.'

Then he turned to Vasanthi and took her hands into his, 'Come on, let's get the operation over with and rest here for a few days. The hospital is opposite the Alps and at least you can enjoy the view as you recover. We'll fly back to London once you feel better.'

Vasanthi agreed reluctantly.

While being wheeled into the operation theatre, she said, 'Don't tell anyone about this in Bangalore or Mysore, especially your mother. She'll worry about her Munna and may run here to help you look after me. I'm sure I'll be all right soon.'

She smiled and Mukesh nervously watched her disappear into the operation area.

2

Phone Calls

Mukesh's cell phone rang. It was John, his colleague. He said, 'Mack, our next project is delayed. I thought that I'd let you know so that you don't have to hurry back to London. Let's meet whenever you get here.'

'Okay, thanks.'

Just after he hung up, he got another call. It was Neeraja. 'Munna, Appa has had a heart attack and he's in the ICU. Come home quickly.'

For a minute, Mukesh was taken aback. How could this happen to his father? And how could he leave Vasanthi alone? Neeraja said, 'Munna, can you hear me?'

'Akka, I can hear you clearly. I'm in Lausanne, not London. Vasanthi and I came here to ski and, unfortunately, she met with an accident just a few hours ago. Right now, she's in the operation theatre. I'll check the flight times and leave as quickly as I can. How's Appa? What does the doctor say?'

Neeraja replied, 'Wait, I'll call you back in two minutes.' She disconnected the call.

Mukesh immediately decided on his plan of action. After the operation, he would catch the first flight to Bangalore the next day. He knew that Vasanthi would understand why he had to see his father, but he wanted somebody to be with her till he came back. He was not sure if her sisters already had the required visa for travel. His friends in London may not be able to come at such short notice either. Suddenly, he thought of John and phoned him, 'John, I have to travel to India unexpectedly to see my sick father. Do you think that you can come and help Vasanthi out for a few days till the doctors allow her to go back to London? Once she's at home, she'll manage things on her own.'

John replied, 'That's not a problem, Mack! I'll reach Lausanne tonight or tomorrow morning.'

'Thank you so much, John!'

Now that that was settled, Mukesh's thoughts turned towards his father, 'Neeraja wouldn't have asked me to come if it wasn't serious. Will I be able to see Appa one last time? What if something happens to him before I reach Bangalore?'

The phone rang again. It was not Neeraja this time, it was his mother. Sumati said, 'Munna, the doctor informed us that he can't say anything right now. It'll give me confidence if you can come here. Bring Vasanthi also.'

'She's met with a small accident and won't be able to make the trip, but I'm coming. Don't worry. Please wait for me, Amma. Please.'

He heard Sumati sobbing as he ended the call.

An hour later, Vasanthi was wheeled out of surgery and brought to her room. She was conscious and able to talk despite the medications. Mukesh went near her and put a hand on her shoulder, 'I just got a call from India. Appa is not well.'

'What happened?' she asked, immediately concerned.

He told her about his father. Without a moment's hesitation, she said, 'Leave for Bangalore immediately, Mukesh. Don't worry about me. I'm sure that your mother will be feeling helpless without you. You should be with her at this time.'

Her words gave him encouragement and reassurance. He went back to the hotel and started packing his bags.

~

When Mukesh entered the first-class cabin of the airplane, he hardly noticed anyone. He was busy remembering when he had last seen Appa.

It had been the first day of the new year and his father had given him ten thousand pounds as a gift. Mukesh had felt awkward and said, 'Appa, I'm an adult now. You don't have to celebrate my birthday like I'm a child.'

Rao Saheb, being a man of few words, had simply said, 'You'll always be a child to me, Munna.'

His parents celebrated two dates as his birthday every year—one was New Year's Day and the other was Buddha Purnima. When Mukesh was still a child, he often asked his mother, 'Why do I have two birthdays, Amma?'

She would affectionately hug him and say, 'When you were very small, we were buying some vegetables on the road. Suddenly, you pulled your hand away from mine and ran across the road. Before I could grab you, a truck hit you. Luckily, you rolled away and fell on the other side of the road, away from the truck. Munna, you could have died that day! But it was Buddha Purnima, and you survived. That was God's gift to me and a rebirth for you.'

Since that day, Sumati had fed orphans and children in a blind school and also performed a puja for Mukesh every year on Buddha Purnima.

For a second, Mukesh was terrified thinking of a world without his father. Unconsciously, his hand went to his sacred thread or *janeu*. After his thread ceremony, when he was eight years old, Sumati had told him, 'Whenever you are scared, touch the thread and recite the Gayatri mantra. You will get the strength to face all your problems. And remember, never ever remove the janeu or the chain around your neck.'

'Amma, why can't I remove the chain?' he had asked.

'Because I say so. I believe the chain protects you from harm and negativity.'

Suddenly, his eyes filled with tears thinking about his parents and their unconditional love. He was unable to sleep even as he leaned back and closed his eyes.

3

The Outsider

When Mukesh reached Bangalore and turned his cell phone back on, he found an email from Vasanthi. She was going back to London the next day.

He walked out of the airport and ran into his parents' driver Shafi, who was waiting for him near the exit. Mukesh saw Shafi's face and knew at once that his Appa was no more. His voice dropped to a whisper, 'When did it happen?'

'Early this morning.'

By the time they reached home, the house was filled with people and Mukesh barely managed to squeeze through the doorway. When he saw his father's lifeless body on the floor covered in white, he broke down and could not hold back his tears. He held his father's feet and sobbed uncontrollably. Slowly, he became aware of a gentle hand on his shoulder. He turned around to see Sumati through his tears. For the first time in his life, he saw his mother losing control too. He grabbed her hand and hugged her tightly as if nothing could separate them. Their sorrow was inconsolable.

Neeraja came into the room and hugged her mother and brother. Mukesh felt like he had lost the roof over his head and that he'd become an orphan. Nobody could ever replace Appa. Time would pass and he'd get used to living without his father's presence, but the irreparable loss was going to stay with him forever. His family would always be incomplete now.

After a few minutes, the pandit came to him and said, 'You must shave your head and perform your father's final rites.'

Mukesh nodded. Though he did not believe in all the rituals or the need to shave his head, he knew it would bring a sense of peace to his mother and he was ready to do anything to make her happy.

Some time later, people started asking the family, 'Where's Vasanthi? Why hasn't she come?'

Neither Mukesh nor Sumati bothered to respond.

A few hours later, the six-foot Rao Saheb was consigned to the flames and soon, he turned into three handfuls of ashes. The next day, Mukesh immersed the ashes in the river Kaveri and prayed for his father's departed soul.

Soon, all their relatives and friends left and Neeraja,

Mukesh and Sumati remained at home. Neeraja's husband, Satish, went to the grocery store nearby. The house seemed quiet and listless.

Mukesh brought out a large picture of Rao Saheb and garlanded it with flowers. The man who was alive just a week ago had become a static two-dimensional picture.

Sumati came and stood next to him. She said gently, 'Munna, now that all the ceremonies are over, go back and take care of Vasanthi. You can come back on the eleventh day for the remaining rituals.'

But Mukesh wanted to be with his mother at this time. He phoned Vasanthi who was back in London. She insisted that he stay back in India and told her mother-in-law, 'Amma, you need him more. I'm doing fine here.' Mukesh thanked God for the two amazing and understanding women that he had been blessed with.

Mukesh was looking online for a return ticket to London for two weeks later when his brother-in-law, Satish, returned and asked him unexpectedly, 'Do you know if your father has left a will?'

Mukesh turned to Sumati, 'Do you know, Amma?'

Her eyes welled up with tears and she replied, 'Yes, Munna. Your father made a will and kept it with our family advocate, Mr Joshi. They've known each other forever and your Appa trusted him.'

He nodded. Yes, he remembered Uncle Joshi and Appa spending a lot of time together.

'Can we call him?' asked Satish curiously.

Mukesh and Neeraja did not really care and went back to whatever they were doing.

Sumati looked at Satish. He was a good-looking, tall and shrewd man. He had met Neeraja during her MBA at the university campus during his visit there for an inter-college debate. A mutual friend had introduced them and within a year, Satish had proposed marriage to Neeraja. She had first broken the news to Mukesh and he, in turn, had conveyed it to their parents.

A few days after that, Rao Saheb and Sumati had gone to Satish's house. Appa had not liked the boy's parents. Satish's father was an ordinary clerk in an office and the family was not financially sound. They just about managed to get by. Rao Saheb had felt uneasy when Satish's father had asked for a big fat wedding and flight tickets for almost sixty of his relatives. The entire meeting had been about money, gold and property.

When Rao Saheb had mentioned his reluctance to Mukesh, he had tried to pacify his father, 'Appa, we must understand. Satish's family comes from a deprived background. It matters a lot to them to get an educated daughter-in-law from a wealthy background.'

'No, *beta*, that's not true,' his father had said. 'I don't come from a rich family either, but for me, the individual is more important than money.'

'Everyone's different, Appa. Besides, Neeru loves Satish.

He seems to be an intelligent boy; maybe he can understand and take care of such frivolous demands in the future. Let's go ahead with it for her sake.'

A few months later, Neeraja had been married with pomp and fanfare. Rao Saheb had gifted her a bungalow, gold ornaments and money so that she would not have to depend on anyone.

Sumati sighed at the memory. Her husband had taken care of everything!

'So, when can we call him?' repeated Satish.

'If you think that it's necessary, please go ahead and do so,' replied Sumati, feeling slightly uncomfortable at his eagerness to see the will.

Satish picked up his cell phone and requested Mr Joshi to come to their house.

The next day, in the afternoon, Mr Joshi asked the entire family to join him in the living room and closed the door so that they could discuss things freely. Satish said, 'I think I'll wait outside. This is the family's personal business.'

Mukesh stopped him, 'You are a part of the family too. Please stay.'

Satish sat down without a word.

Mr Joshi opened the will and began reading. After a few minutes, Mukesh interrupted him, 'Uncle, I'm afraid that I don't understand much of the legalese. I'm sure that Appa would have done everything properly. Please tell us just the main points.'

Mr Joshi replied, 'Okay, Munna. I'll tell you everything in brief. The fixed deposits in the bank have been divided into equal halves to be shared between your mother and Neeru. Sumati gets all the gold in the locker as well as this house. It is her prerogative to write a will and split her share as she sees fit.'

'What's the total amount of money in the bank?' asked Satish.

'Around two crores.'

'What about the remaining assets?' probed Satish.

'The coffee plantation in Coorg, the house in Delhi, the other residence in Bangalore and the business goes to Munna. The driver Shafi and the helper Ramlal get ten lakh rupees each. The cook Radha gets five lakhs and the gardener Mahadev gets two lakhs. Your father wants to give twenty-five lakhs to the orphanage in Jayanagar and another ten to the Raghavendra Swami temple. Neeru gets to keep all the gifts, including the bungalow, that were given to her during her wedding.'

There was silence in the room.

Satish complained, 'This is unfair. I never imagined that Rao Saheb would do such a thing.'

'It's what he wanted,' said Mr Joshi. 'Besides, Sumati can decide what she wants to do with her share at a later date.'

'What's the approximate value of the remaining assets?'

Mr Joshi was a seasoned lawyer. He answered tactfully,

'You used to help him with the business, Satish. You should have a better idea.'

Mukesh wondered out loud, 'Why did Appa leave so much for me?'

Mr Joshi realized that it was time to give the family some space. He stood up, 'Money matters are always complex. It is better to resolve them calmly. The four of you need to sit down and discuss this as a family.' He turned to Mukesh and said, 'Munna, I need the power of attorney document from your Dad's files to settle some of these matters. Call me after you have located it.'

'Okay, Uncle.'

After he had left, Mukesh asked his sister, 'Neeru, do you know where we should look? I don't know where Appa kept his legal papers.'

Sumati replied absent-mindedly, 'All his important papers are inside the old safe in the study upstairs.'

When Rao Saheb was alive, nobody was allowed to touch the old-fashioned safe that was originally purchased in Delhi. It was his first purchase when he was branching out on his own. He had remained attached to it and considered it lucky for business.

Neeraja went to her father's study on the second floor and Mukesh headed to his bedroom wondering why Appa had been partial to him. Was it because he was a boy? He shrugged off the thought instantly, knowing very well that that was not the case. Maybe if he gave some of his assets to Neeraja, it would appease Satish and things could go back to normal.

Mukesh dozed off.

He awoke with a start to the sound of sobbing coming from his mother's room. He ran there and found Neeraja and Amma crying on the bed. Satish was standing and looking upset while holding a picture in his hand. Mukesh knew why his brother-in-law was hurt—Satish thought that Appa had divided the assets unfairly. Gently, Mukesh told him, 'Neeru and I are family and it doesn't matter who gets more. I'll give half of whatever Appa gave me to Neeru. Let's not inconvenience Amma in any way.'

Satish retorted, 'Actually, these assets don't even belong to you. You're not a part of this family.'

'How can you say such a thing?'

'You are not Neeru's real brother,' Satish said slowly. 'You were adopted by this family.'

Mukesh was annoyed, 'This isn't the time to joke around.'

'I'm not joking, Munna. Here, look at this.'

Satish shoved the photograph he was holding into Mukesh's hand. It was an old black-and-white picture of Neeraja and Mukesh sitting on two stools. There was a vase on the left and a curtain painted with waterfalls in the background. Mukesh said, 'I admit that I haven't seen this picture before, but what's so special about it?'

His brother-in-law observed, 'Neeru is wearing a new

skirt and blouse and you are wearing a very, very old T-shirt and shorts.'

'So? What's wrong with that?'

'Look behind the picture.'

Mukesh turned the picture around and saw a handwritten date at the back—'2 February 1980, Picture Palace, Jalna, Maharashtra'.

Immediately, Satish started asking him questions like the lawyer that he was. 'Munna, Neeru's birthday is on 31 December. Can you tell me the year of her birth?'

'1977.'

'And yours?'

'I am two years younger than her,' replied Mukesh.

'Give me the exact date, please.'

'1 January 1980. I remember because Appa and Amma celebrated Neeru's birthday and mine together at midnight on New Year's Eve. But Amma also celebrated my birthday on Buddha Purnima. Why are you bringing this up now?' Mukesh asked sadly.

'Munna, if you were born in the same year that this picture was taken, you should have been one month old in this photograph. Tell me, do you look like a newborn here?' Satish's voice was victorious.

Mukesh stared at the picture. Satish was right. Both Neeraja and he appeared to be two years old—almost the same age.

Satish continued, 'If we consider this picture to be

factually correct, then the two of you must be twins. But you aren't, are you? Neeru has a birth certificate that says that she was born in Vani Vilas Hospital in Bangalore. What about you?'

'Amma told me that I was born at home. She knows my date of birth.' Mukesh turned to Neeraja and asked, 'Akka, where did you find this photograph that's threatening to ruin our relationship?'

Satish smiled. He had made his point.

4

The Shattering Secret

When Neeraja had entered her father's second-floor study earlier, she had opened the safe but had not found the power of attorney document inside. She had thought of calling out to Mukesh to come and help her look in the cupboards, but then had decided against it. She felt sorry for her brother because he was going to have to travel soon and take a long flight back to London. After a twenty-minute search with no luck, she had gone back and looked at the safe again. She had stretched out her hand inside and to her surprise, had found the document and a small box at the back of the safe.

Neeraja had kept the document aside and had curiously opened the box to find a small envelope that had turned yellow with age. She had peeked inside and pulled out a picture—a picture of Mukesh and herself. It was a rare childhood photograph that she had never seen before. Without even closing the safe, she had run down to show the picture to her mother. She had met her husband on the staircase and cried out in excitement, 'Satish, look what I found inside the safe! It's Munna and me. Don't we look cute together? Amma and Appa must have forgotten about it.'

Suddenly, she had remembered that she had left the safe open upstairs. She had told her husband, 'Here, take this picture down and show it to Amma. I'll close the safe and join the two of you in a minute.'

Satish had nodded as Neeraja walked back upstairs. He had started climbing down the stairs while looking at the picture. In a flash, he had noticed that his wife and her brother looked like they were of the same age. Something was wrong. He had thought, 'Neeru looks just like her mother—the curly hair and the straight nose are definitely from her. Munna is also tall like Rao Saheb but his features are very different. He has dark, soft and straight hair but Rao Saheb was completely bald. Still, it is difficult to tell from anyone's external appearance. I shouldn't jump to conclusions.'

Satish was a smart man and had realized that his mother-in-law would know the truth. He had gone to Sumati's bedroom and stood near the door. Absent-mindedly, he had noticed the photos on her dressing table—one of Mukesh's marriage and the other of Neeraja's and his.

Sumati was formal with her son-in-law and had been surprised to see him at her door. She had stood up.

He had come inside and asked her, 'When was Munna born?'

Neeraja had also come in a few seconds behind him.

'You have been my son-in-law for the last five years now. You know when we celebrate Munna's birthday,' Sumati had said.

'That's why I'm asking you.' Satish had held out the photograph. 'You took this in Jalna.'

Sumati had looked at the picture and felt the blood drain right out of her. She had turned pale and asked him, 'Where did you find this?'

Neeraja had replied, 'It was tucked away at the back of Appa's safe in an old envelope.'

Satish had interrupted, 'Amma, Neeru's future depends on this. Is Munna not your son? Or is Neeru really not your biological daughter?'

Sumati had not responded.

Neeraja, taken aback, had started crying, 'Am I not your daughter? Tell me, Amma!'

Sumati had still not answered the question. She had also begun sobbing. Their cries had woken up Mukesh, who had then walked into the bedroom and found his mother and sister crying on the bed.

~

Sumati felt exhausted. After a few deep breaths, she said, 'Neeru is my daughter and Munna is my adopted son. I love him more than my life itself.'

Satish smirked. Neeraja could not believe her ears while Mukesh felt like the earth had just opened up and swallowed him whole.

A few minutes passed and the world seemed to be at a standstill.

Satish left the room. Mukesh stared at the cowshed outside the window. A calf was drinking its mother's milk. Amma was crying. Slowly, he went near her and sat in front of her on the floor. 'Amma, tell me that this is a lie and that you're playing a prank,' he said.

Sumati did not reply but placed a hand on his head.

'Why didn't you tell me earlier?' Mukesh asked.

'Munna, we both loved you like you were our own. So there was no reason for us to tell you.'

'But Appa shared almost everything with me. He was one of my best friends. Why did he hide this from me?'

'Munna, Appa wanted to tell you many times but I stopped him from doing so. Before he went into a coma, he called out your name. He must have felt that you should know what had happened.'

Mukesh was a little upset, 'Why didn't you let him tell me the truth?'

'Because of fear. I was scared, Munna. I'd heard from many people that once a child learns that he is adopted, he goes in search of his biological parents and forgets about everyone else. I was scared that you'd leave and forget about me, too. What would I do then?'

'Amma, where did you find me—in an orphanage or in a dustbin?'

Sumati shook her head, 'No, not from an orphanage, beta. Neither did we find you in a dustbin. Your mother gave you to me.'

'Who is she? And where is she?'

'Her name is Rupinder Kaur and she lives in Amritsar.'

'Amma, why did she give me away? Am I a sardar?'

She sighed, 'It's a long story.'

~

Sumati recounted that Rao Saheb's family was from a village near Kunigal, which was close to Bangalore. Krishna Rao had completed his tenth grade, but due to financial reasons, he could not study further and found a job as an ordinary clerk in the goods division in the railways. He had taken care of getting his seven sisters married since his father had passed away when he was very young. By the time it was his turn, nobody had wanted to give their daughter to a man who had nothing to offer his wife. Then someone had suggested Sumati's name. She was an orphan who was living with her brother and his family and they were even poorer than Krishna Rao.

Soon, they were married in a temple and lived happily in Bangalore. After fifteen months of marriage, Sumati became pregnant. At the time of delivery, she was rushed to the government hospital in Bangalore, where she gave birth to Neeru. Due to complications during the delivery, the doctor decided to do an emergency hysterectomy and remove her uterus. The couple felt very sad that they could not have more children, but they decided to not tell any of their relatives about the operation and to give their daughter the best life that they could. Later, when Krishna's mother learnt that the newborn was a girl, she did not even come to see her grandchild despite being in the same city. Instead, she sent a message to Krishna and Sumati that they should have a baby boy the following year.

After a few months, Krishna was transferred to Jalna, a railway junction in Maharashtra. The couple was very happy to leave Bangalore because of Krishna's mother's constant taunting. When they reached Jalna, Krishna was allotted a single-roomed house in the railway colony in front of the station.

Sumati adjusted easily since she had learnt Hindi in school and settled into a routine very quickly.

The only problem she had was that of procuring drinking water. The water came just for an hour very early in the morning and sometimes, she could not get up in time to fill the buckets. One day, her neighbour told her, 'If you need water urgently, cross the road and go to the Sardarji's big bungalow. The old lady in the house is a tough woman, but her daughter-in-law is nice and she will let you take some water from their well.'

One day, Sumati had no water at home. Hesitantly, she approached the Sardarji's house for the first time with Neeru in tow. She found a young woman cleaning the vessels at the back of the house. Sumati asked her timidly, 'May I take a bucket of water from your well?'

'Why are you feeling shy? Please come and take it,' said the woman and pointed to the well which was a few feet away.

Suddenly, Sumati heard an authoritative voice from the balcony, 'Who is it, Rupinder?'

'A woman from the railway colony has come with her child. She wants a bucket of water.'

The old lady said in Punjabi, 'Okay, give her water. You should never refuse someone asking for water. But tell her not to make it an everyday habit.'

Sumati did not understand what was being said.

Rupinder smiled and said in Hindi, 'Please feel free to take water whenever you want.'

While she was pulling the bucket of water out from the well, Neeru stood behind her mother holding the *pallu* of her sari.

Rupinder asked, 'Is she your daughter?'

'Yes. Do you have children too?'

'One son.'

Just then, a young boy a little shorter than Neeru came out from the bushes with a piece of chapatti in his hand. Rupinder smiled, 'He's my son.'

The boy felt awkward in front of the unexpected visitors and ran to his mother's side. Neeru was holding a laddu in her hand and immediately went to him and gave him half of it. At first, the boy was hesitant to take it. Sumati encouraged him, 'Take it, beta. She's your akka.'

'What does "akka" mean?'

'In our language, it means elder sister,' said Sumati. 'What's your name, beta?'

'I am Munna,' the boy said.

Neeru repeated, 'Munna.'

~

'Amma, I am that boy, am I not?'

Mukesh's voice brought Sumati back to the present, 'Yes, Munna.'

'Isn't that why I call you Amma and Neeru Akka?'

With tears in their eyes, Neeraja and Mukesh looked at each other. Satish would never understand the feelings of being together for a lifetime or the fond memories of their first meeting. Neeraja had shared her laddu with Munna and Munna had shared his chapatti with her.

With a trembling hand and tears flowing down her cheeks, Neeraja went to her brother, held his hand and simply said, 'Munna.'

5

For a Better Life

In a short time, Neeru and Munna became inseparable.

Rupinder and Munna came to Sumati's house every afternoon, but Neeru never went to Munna's house to play. Sometimes, Rupinder would leave Munna in Sumati's house from morning till night. Frequently, he'd even sleep over and not go back to his house at all. He quickly learnt Kannada and started calling Sumati 'Amma' and Krishna 'Appa'. Sumati's obvious love and Krishna's affection for Munna made Rupinder very happy and sad at the same time.

Slowly, Sumati found out more about Rupinder. She was a hard-working girl from a poor family that lived in a village on the border of Haryana and Punjab. When she was very young, she was married to Surinder—a school dropout and a short-tempered man who was completely controlled by his mother. She made Rupinder work like a servant all day. Surinder's family was a big and rich joint family in Jalna. Everybody stayed together in a huge house and worked in the family business.

Within a year of her marriage, the joint family opted to separate and Surinder decided to start a car workshop along with his brother. A few months later, Munna was born, just before the opening of the shop. He had a dark patch on his right foot and Surinder's mother was convinced that it was a bad omen. As if to prove her correct, the workshop did not do well. The mother-in-law started ignoring Munna completely and only paid attention to Surinder's brother's children. Even as a child, Munna felt the rejection and preferred to stay in Sumati's house.

Months passed. The family decided to sell the bungalow and go to Amritsar to try their luck there. Rupinder started crying as she told Sumati about the family's plans. Sumati consoled her, 'Rupinder, please don't cry. We too are transferred every two or three years due to my husband's job in the railways. You will find good friends everywhere because you are a nice lady. At the very least, you will be closer to your maternal home and can visit your parents often.'

Rupinder replied, 'That's not the problem. My problem is that my mother-in-law doesn't want Munna to come with us to Amritsar. She says that he'll bring bad luck to the family over there too. She wants me to send him to my parents' house in the village. My parents are old and poor and if Munna lives there, he won't get a good education and will end up becoming a labourer or something like that when he grows up. My husband doesn't listen to me either. I don't know what to do.'

Sumati did not have an answer, but she could understand the mindset of the older generation. Her own mother-in-law had refused to come to Jalna to meet Neeru though they had requested her several times and even sent her a railway pass. Sumati sympathized with Rupinder. The poor woman had no support from her maternal home, no money, no power, and a useless husband. The only positive thing in her life was her love for her son.

Rupinder stood up to go home but Munna was sleeping next to Neeru under an old bedsheet. She was about to lift him and carry him home when Sumati said, 'Let him sleep here tonight. God knows how much longer you'll be here. Let them enjoy each other's company till then.'

The next day, Sumati found three rupees while she was cleaning the house. She was very happy to find some extra cash. She thought about taking Munna and Neeru's picture in the reasonably priced and popular photo studio called Picture Palace, before Rupinder departed from Jalna. Enthusiastically, she shared her plan with Rupinder and asked for her permission: 'I want to take the kids to the city for a photograph. They can keep it as a souvenir of the time they've spent together.'

Rupinder was in no mood to refuse. She had other things to worry about.

That afternoon, Sumati and Krishna took the two children to the city. All of them felt excited when they walked into the studio. Krishna held Munna's hand and Sumati held Neeru's. When they inquired, they were told that the photo would cost two rupees. Sumati and Krishna had the children pose for the photograph. After the picture was taken, the four of them went out into the street and ate bhelpuri with the remaining money. It was a big treat for Neeru and Munna.

When Sumati went back to drop Munna, Rupinder updated her, 'This time, my husband's family wants to start a grocery store in a large chowk in Amritsar near the Mata Lal Devi temple. They've located a corner site and think that a grocery shop there will be extremely profitable, especially since it is next to a school. We will live upstairs and open the shop downstairs.'

Within a few months, the site was purchased and everything was finalized. The family was going to leave in a few days. But Rupinder was worried about her son and shared her thoughts with Sumati, 'How can I leave Munna with my parents? They can't take care of him and nobody is listening to me. I am ready to give him away to someone who will adopt him and keep him well, instead of sending him to that village. Murder and theft is rampant there and the children can't study properly because of the bad environment. Munna won't have a future without a good education.'

Rupinder wept in despair.

That night, Sumati talked to Krishna before going to bed, 'You know that we can't have another child. What do you think about us adopting Munna?'

Krishna was surprised at her suggestion, 'Why will they give their child to us? We are from a different community and culture. Besides, Rupinder may change her mind in a few days. Think about it: what future will Munna have in our house? We aren't rich like Rupinder's family.'

Sumati countered, 'We can educate him and treat him the way we treat Neeru. I know stitching very well. I am willing to make clothes at home and supplement the family income. But no matter what, we'll give our best to both the kids. It's better that he stays with us rather than becoming a coolie in a village far away. If you agree, I'll talk to Rupinder about it. If she refuses, it's the end of the matter anyway. But tell me, do you have any objection?'

Krishna smiled, 'You know how much I love Munna. I've never differentiated between Neeru and him.'

Both of them had a restless night.

In the morning, Krishna placed his hand affectionately on his wife's shoulder, 'Sumati, I support you wholeheartedly. Don't ask me about this again. We've made the decision together. But I worry that once we have him, I won't be able to give him up.'

Sumati felt the tears welling up in her eyes.

At noon, she went to Rupinder's house and found her busy packing. Sumati told her directly, 'I want to talk to you about something important. Come to my house when you can.'

Without asking, Munna followed Sumati back to her home. When he saw Neeru, he squealed in delight and they started playing.

Rupinder joined them half an hour later. She told Sumati, 'We are leaving in two days.'

'What have you decided about Munna?'

'My husband says that if I don't leave him in my parents' home, we can leave him in a gurdwara orphanage.' Rupinder almost broke down.

'If you don't mind, may I suggest something?'

'Anything. Please tell me. I'm ready to do anything that'll make Munna's life better,' pleaded Rupinder.

'Can we adopt him?'

Rupinder stared at her.

Sumati repeated, 'Can we please adopt him?'

This time, Rupinder understood. 'Are you sure? Have you asked your husband?'

'Of course. We've taken this decision together. But we have one condition. After a few years have passed and Munna has settled down with us, you can't take him away. It won't be good for him and we won't be able to let him go either.'

Rupinder thought for a few minutes. 'No, I won't ask for him once he's living with you.'

'You may not ask, but your mother-in-law or husband may come back one day just because he's a boy. They place a lot of importance on having a male heir.'

'I'm sure that they won't ask. Munna's future is with me, not with them,' she said firmly.

'How can I believe you? Rupinder, please talk to everyone at home and then decide.'

'Believe me, Sumati, they won't look back at Munna once he is gone. I promise you and swear on Wahe Guru as a witness that we won't come back for him. Not only that, I guarantee you that I won't even visit him. It'll be very hard for me, but I want Munna to have stability in his life. That's more important.' Rupinder paused. 'But what will happen if you have another baby later? I know that you'll take care of Munna well, but once you have your own boy, then things might change.'

Sumati sighed, 'I can't have another child because I had a hysterectomy right after Neeru was born. Only my husband and I know about it.'

Rupinder held her hand and sobbed, 'Give him a good education and raise him to be a good human being. Knowing you, I'm sure that you will do that anyway.' Though she was crying, Rupinder felt a sense of satisfaction and relief knowing that Munna would have a good future.

Sumati said, 'I pray to the Guru to give you strength.

Do you want my husband to come and talk to your family about Munna?'

'No, that's not needed. They just want to be rid of him, you know that.' She looked at Sumati. 'But I want to keep Munna with me till the day we leave.'

Sumati nodded.

Rupinder took Munna and went home.

Two days went past in a flash. The day Rupinder was leaving, she came to Sumati's house carrying Munna in her arms. Her eyes were swollen and it looked like she'd been crying continuously. Munna was wearing new clothes and carrying a candy box and a new toy. He had no idea that this was the last time he was seeing his mother. He saw Neeru and scrambled down from his mother's arms to play with her.

'Sumati, today may be our last meeting. I don't know whether I'm doing right or wrong, but I'm giving my dear baby to you. I have a bad mother-in-law, an alcoholic husband and a bickering family. Munna doesn't have any future with us. It's better that he stay with you.'

Her friend nodded.

Rupinder removed a gold chain from her neck and put it around Munna's. She said, 'Sumati, this is the only gift my parents gave me when I was married. I don't have any money to give, but this must always be with Munna. Don't ever tell him about me, unless it's a matter of life and death.'

Sumati gave her a hug, 'Before you leave, tell me, what's his date of birth?'

'I don't know the date, but he was born on Buddha Purnima a year and a half ago. On his birthday, please donate food to the poor, Sumati. That's the only way to celebrate.'

Sobbing, Rupinder turned and left the house.

6

A Son's Right

By the time the story was over, it was late at night. Sumati was exhausted and stressed. The thirty-year-old secret was finally out. She said, 'Munna, now you know the whole truth.'

Mukesh kept his head on her lap. He knew that she would not hide anything from him. The fear of losing her son and the promise that she had given Rupinder had stopped her from telling him. She had kept her promise and loved him like her own. She'd encouraged him to study further and supported him when he wanted to marry Vasanthi. How many parents did that much even for their biological children?

'Amma, Appa and you have done so much for me. Otherwise, God alone knows where I might have been,' Mukesh said.

'Munna, your father loved you a lot. He used to call you our lucky star.'

'What do you mean?'

Sumati was thrown back into the past again.

~

Within a month of Rupinder leaving, Krishna was transferred to Delhi. Munna asked for his mother every day, but once the family relocated to Delhi, he became fascinated with the new surroundings and adjusted quickly. Krishna was not able to get a house in the railway colony since Delhi was a big and crowded city. So the family rented a small house on the outskirts.

Life was difficult but Sumati was happy. Munna was not as tall as Neeru, so she told everyone that she had two children—a girl and a younger boy. Now, Sumati thought about introducing Munna to her parents-in-law's family. She told her husband, 'If we tell your family that we have adopted Munna, then whenever we visit Bangalore, there's a chance of someone telling him that he's not from our community or that he was adopted. Or maybe they'll treat him differently from Neeru and he will figure it out on his own. Please let me do as I think is right.'

Krishna did not really agree but allowed her to go ahead with her plan.

Sumati wrote a letter to her parents-in-law and her

brother telling them that she was six months pregnant. She knew that neither her sister-in-law nor Krishna's mother would offer to come and help her in Delhi for the delivery or invite her to come and stay in Bangalore. She was right. After three months, she informed them that she had had a baby boy on 1 January 1980. When her mother-in-law learnt that she had a grandson, she wrote to Sumati blessing her and the child and thanking her for the continuation of the family name. Meanwhile, Sumati decided that she would not visit Bangalore for a few years.

Unexpectedly, Krishna's mother passed away in a few months and he had to go to Bangalore to perform her last rites. Krishna told his relatives that Sumati could not come because of their infant child. This is how their last connection with Bangalore was severed.

Munna and Neeru grew up to be healthy toddlers under the close supervision of their parents.

Now that Sumati had some time, she decided to buy a sewing machine and stitch clothes. However, they did not have any extra money or even gold jewellery that they could sell. One day, she told Krishna, 'Please mortgage Munna's gold chain and buy a sewing machine.'

Krishna objected, 'We can't do that. The chain is Rupinder's gift to her son and we have no right over it.'

'I didn't tell you to sell it—only to mortgage it.'

'What will happen if we can't pay back the mortgage? Then we will lose the chain, Sumati. It's our responsibility.'

Sumati was courageous and practical. She said confidently, 'I'll work hard to repay the mortgage money and get the chain back. I know how important Rupinder's gift is.'

Various moneylenders told Krishna, 'We are willing to buy your chain for ten thousand rupees. Why don't you sell it?'

'No, Sir. This chain is given to my son with special blessings. We can't sell it,' Krishna said.

He managed to mortgage the chain and Sumati bought a sewing machine. Munna performed the machine puja before his mother began stitching. Since their neighbourhood was a relatively poor one, Sumati kept her charges minimal—two rupees per blouse, one rupee per skirt, and so on. She herself went from door to door to collect the cloth material. She stitched the clothes on time and returned the remaining cloth. Her honesty and skill made her popular and she was able to get the chain back within a year.

The next year, she mortgaged the chain again and repeated the process. The orders grew slowly but surely and within three years, she had three sewing machines and two helpers. Munna and Neeru also helped her with the household chores. She truly believed that Munna had brought luck to the family.

Soon, the two children started going to school. On the first day of school, Sumati performed Saraswati Puja for them and registered their names. Since she did not know Munna's real name, Krishna and she thought about it and agreed that Mukesh was a wonderful name because they were both fans of the singer Mukesh. Thus Munna was named Mukesh K. Rao and his date of birth became 1 January 1980, while his sister was registered as Neeraja K. Rao, born on 31 December 1977.

Three years later, Krishna passed a departmental exam and became a commercial goods clerk in the railways. In this role, he met many traders from Delhi and other places. One of them was Keshav Lal, the transport manager of Vibhavari Garments in Delhi's Lajpat Nagar market. The store exported garments to other nations and supplied bales of cloth to various parts of the country through the goods trains. Normally, whenever the consignment arrived or reached its destination, Krishna's boss informed Lal, who immediately sent his employees to take delivery of the shipment. Every Diwali and New Year, Keshav Lal came to the railway goods division to give special gifts to Krishna's boss and a few other senior people. Krishna usually got just a box of sweets.

On a rare rainy day during winter, the consignment of Vibhavari Garments landed in Delhi a day earlier than scheduled and was stashed away in an open and unsecured yard. Krishna's boss was on vacation so nobody made the call to Keshav Lal. Though it was not his responsibility, Krishna covered the goods with plastic sheets and called

Lal, who came at once to take delivery. He was happy to see the consignment in perfect condition. With tears in his eyes, he said, 'Mr Rao, I will never forget your help. If the consignment had been stolen or drenched, my company would have incurred huge losses and I would have lost my job. I am extremely grateful to you.'

'It's simply my duty,' said Krishna.

The next day, Keshav Lal came to Krishna's house with a big box of *mithai*. In the veranda, he saw three sewing machines and some people busy stitching. Since he was in the cloth business, he sat down and checked the quality of the garments. When he met the couple, he said to Krishna, 'Mr Rao, if your wife can supply clothes to us, I can give her some contract work at a decent rate. I've checked some of her work and it's good.'

Krishna turned to look at Sumati, who smiled and nodded, 'I'll try my best.'

When Mukesh and Neeraja came back from school, they were very happy to see the big box of mithai.

Slowly, Sumati increased the number of machines to five and the number of helpers to three. Eventually, she became the manager and the rest was history. Sumati's business grew exponentially with each passing year. Krishna also took an interest in her business and began managing the administrative work and odd jobs. Within a few years, he resigned from his job and started Mukesh Exports.

Time flew. The family bought a house in the esteemed

Defence Colony. Sumati took her children to Bangalore by air and performed Mukesh's thread ceremony there. She gave her sisters-in-law very expensive gifts.

Soon, Krishna Rao learnt the tricks of the trade and started exporting heavily. He came to be known as Rao Saheb. The family expanded the business with a new factory in Bangalore and relocated there. Still, Rao Saheb and Sumati retained the Delhi office.

~

Listening to his mother, Mukesh finally understood his father's will. Rao Saheb, being the man that he was, knew that Sumati and he were able to start the garments business because of the gold chain. But the chain was never theirs to begin with; it was always Mukesh's. That's why he had left the business to him. Rao Saheb could have willed at least half to Neeraja, but he did not.

Mukesh recalled an incident when he had gone to his friend's house for a sleepover many, many years ago. The next morning, he had taken the chain off before having a bath and forgotten it on the bathroom counter beside the sink. When he had come home, his mother had been busy telling somebody to make ten gold mangalsutras to donate for community marriages and had not noticed the missing chain.

However, her eyes had gone to his neck during lunch

that day and her face had instantly turned pale. 'Munna, where's the chain?' she had demanded.

'I think I left it in Rakesh's house. I'll pick it up tomorrow.'

'Stop eating! Go and bring the chain right now,' she had ordered him.

'Relax, Amma. It must be on the bathroom counter. It's not going anywhere. I'll call Rakesh and ask him to bring it to our house tomorrow,' he had said.

'No, call your friend and tell him to keep it ready. Go with the driver and pick it up immediately.'

'You donate so much gold to make mangalsutras for poor women. My chain is worth only thirty thousand rupees. Then why are you so attached to this chain? Attachment is not good, Amma.'

Sumati had snapped at him, 'Munna, don't talk to me about attachment. I am ordering you to go and get the chain right now.'

Mukesh had been very upset and had left home to bring the chain back. Upon his return, he had given the chain to his mother and said angrily, 'Rakesh laughed at me when I went there. He said that I was the son of a millionaire and that I came back only for the sake of a measly chain. Amma, I don't want to wear it. If I lose it, then I'm afraid that you'll get a heart attack.'

At the time, Sumati had not said anything. She had simply held the chain in her hands and looked up at the goddess Lakshmi's picture in their living room.

Now, Mukesh knew why. The chain was a parting gift from his biological mother. Though she had looked after him for only a year and a half, she had given him life and breastfed him.

He was disappointed, angry and sad. 'How could my mother give me away to somebody just like that? Why didn't she keep me?'

His mind was not at rest. He felt completely alone and thought, 'Who am I? Why was I born? My biological parents rejected me and gave me away to this family. Though they have treated me as their son, I am not really a part of them. The house, the cars, my education—they are all an obligation. I am an outsider.'

Sumati came close and patted his head again and again, as if to reassure him.

Mukesh remembered Vasanthi and wondered what she would say. 'She's a traditional girl. Will she accept me now? I am the son of a sardar. What will she think of me?'

He wanted to call her and tell her everything. When he phoned her some time later, she asked him how things were going and advised him, 'You're the favourite child of the house. So you must take care of your mother and sister. Don't worry about me. I am managing very well here. Come back after things are settled there.'

'What mother? What sister?' he wanted to say. They did not mean anything to him today, but he could not explain all this to her over the phone. He said goodbye and disconnected the call.

A few days later, it was time for the eleventh-day ceremony. Mukesh was still disturbed by his newly revealed past. He did not know what he was going to do about it. The family pandit came for the rituals and said, 'Munna, get ready. We need to complete the rituals on time because I have two other appointments today.'

Satish ignored Mukesh and went to Sumati, who was standing next to her son. He asked her, 'Tell me, Amma, what rituals should I do?'

Satish was sending a clear message to Mukesh—he did not belong to this family. So what right did he have to do anything for Rao Saheb? Mukesh felt terrible. He wanted to perform his father's rites, not because of the inheritance, but because he still felt like his parents' son, even though the attachment was not biological. He cursed the moment when Neeraja had found the picture. Had that picture remained locked away, life would have gone on as usual.

Mukesh told Sumati firmly, 'Amma, I don't want any money from Appa or you. At least, I know where I come from now. Akka and you can keep my share of the inheritance, but I want to perform Appa's final rituals. It is my right and I will do it for Appa.'

His mother smiled, 'Who said that you aren't going to perform them? Come, sit down. Let's start the ceremony.'

7

Be Careful What You Wish For

After the rituals were completed, the pandit left and the house became quiet.

Two days passed and things remained at a standstill. Sumati wanted Mukesh to move back to India and take charge of the property and the business. She did not trust Satish completely. But she also knew that her son's heart was in the arts and history and he may not be able to handle a business. 'Maybe he can appoint somebody else,' she thought. But she was unable to talk to Mukesh about it because she knew that he was still reeling from the shock of finding out that he was adopted.

However, her son's thoughts were elsewhere. He planned to give his inheritance to Sumati and go back to

London. She could decide what she wanted to do with it. It may be a little difficult for him to live with his limited salary, he thought, but he had been given a good education and that asset was the greatest of them all.

But before returning to London, he wanted to find his biological mother. He was angry. Why had she abandoned him? The question troubled him over and over. Yes, it was very important for him to meet Rupinder. He started packing for Amritsar.

Sumati entered his bedroom and saw that he was planning to leave. Tears glistened in her eyes, 'Beta, where are you going? Don't listen to anyone. Satish doesn't know anything. We have built this company with love and hard work, and we did our best for Neeru and you even when there was no money. We love both of you. Appa's will should be executed the way it is written. I am in agreement with his decision.'

'That's not what I care about, Amma. You are important to me but, right now, I must go to Amritsar and find Rupinder. I want to meet her.'

Sumati was silent for a few minutes. Then she cried out, 'Do you mean to say that you want to go to your real mother? Are you abandoning me, Munna?'

'No, Amma, I'm not. I am just curious about her. Isn't it natural? I promise you that I'll meet her only once.'

Sumati did not reply.

'I need her address, Amma.'

'I haven't had any contact with her over the years but I remember what she had told me. Her family had opened a corner grocery store in a large chowk near the Mata temple. Her husband's name was Surinder and his brother was Parminder.' With a shaky voice she added, 'Rupinder kept you for nine months inside of her. I know that I haven't done that, but I love you as much as she did. She's a fine lady, Munna. Don't get upset with her. She was simply a victim of her unfortunate circumstances. I hope you will forgive her.'

'I will,' said Mukesh.

Early next morning, he flew to Amritsar via Delhi. For the first time since he could remember, he was travelling in economy class. He'd always thought of Delhi as India's capital but now it carried much more significance for him. It was the place where his father had started his business.

It was Mukesh's first visit to Amritsar and he checked in at a reasonably priced hotel. Usually, his father's office took care of his itinerary but he wanted to take care of things on his own this time. Just before noon, he went to the Golden Temple and prayed there, 'Please Wahe Guru, let me find peace during my journey here.'

It was the beginning of summer and the weather was nice, but Mukesh did not even notice. He was wondering where he should start his search. Decades had passed since Sumati and Rupinder had parted. He took an autorickshaw and got off near the Mata Lal Devi temple. After he had walked around for a few minutes, he saw a chowk with a liquor shop at one corner, but there was no grocery store in sight. He entered the shop and found a middle-aged man sitting inside. As soon as he entered, the man stood up and asked, 'What do you want—rum, gin, whisky or beer?'

'No, I don't want anything. I don't eat meat or drink alcohol.' He added, 'Actually, I need information. Two brothers, Parminder and Surinder from Jalna, Maharashtra, opened a grocery store around this area. Have you heard of them? Or are they the owners of this shop?'

'No, beta, the owner of this shop is Harpreet Singh—a young, intelligent, college-educated sardar from Delhi. I'm the store manager here. If you really want more details about this area, I have an uncle who lives nearby. He's been here forever. I can phone him and you can go and talk to him, or I can ask him to come here.'

'No, please don't inconvenience him. I will go to his house.'

The man shouted out to his errand boy and said, 'Take Babuji to Uncle's house and tell him that I have sent this young man.'

Mukesh followed the boy to a house five lanes away. An old sardar was sitting on a green charpoy in the veranda and watching a serial on television. As soon as the errand boy told the old man about the unexpected guest, the sardar called out to his daughter-in-law, 'Bring us something to eat.'

Mukesh was polite, 'Thank you, Sir, but I've had my breakfast already.'

'You have come to a sardar's home. How can you leave without eating anything? It'll be a disgrace on us.'

'Okay, Sir.' Mukesh sat down on a chair near the charpoy and asked him, 'Sir, may I ask how long you've lived around here?'

'Fifty-one years,' he said proudly.

'Have you ever heard of two brothers, Surinder and Parminder, who came from Jalna, Maharashtra? They ran a grocery store here.'

'Yes, I remember them, but for all the wrong reasons. Both of them frequently drank and fought with each other. That's why they lost their shop within a few years. The location of the store was so excellent that anyone with half a brain would have made tons of money, but these two buddhu and short-tempered men ruined their livelihood themselves.'

'What happened to their family?' Mukesh asked.

'First, their old mother died of a heart attack right after the shop was sold. Then Surinder died of cirrhosis, and Parminder and his wife decided to settle down in the wife's village somewhere.'

'What about Surinder? Did he have a family of his own?' Mukesh only wanted to know about Rupinder.

'Yes, yes, he had a wife. But what was her name?' The old man paused, 'Well, I can't recollect right now. Let me ask my wife. She was one of her good friends.'

He called out to his wife, '*Suniye ji*, what was Surinder's wife's name?'

The old woman came out limping and carrying breakfast for the two men, 'Why are you talking about that man? The rascal ruined Rupinder's life.'

Mukesh's heart stopped.

She came and sat next to her husband on the charpoy. She asked Mukesh sharply, 'Who are you? Why do you want to know about that family?'

'I'm a journalist from London but my hometown is Bangalore. My mother was Rupinder's friend when they were younger. I came to Amritsar for some work and she asked me to pay my respects to her.'

'Poor Rupinder,' said the old lady and sighed.

'Why do you say that?' Mukesh was alarmed. 'What happened?'

'Rupinder was treated like a servant in that family. Her mother-in-law was horrible and her husband ill-treated her till the day he died. When their shop closed, Parminder's smart wife took her husband and the money from the sale to her parents' village. Nothing remained with Rupinder. She had no money and no husband. But despite her unhappy life, I was amazed at her unshakeable faith in the divine. She went to Harmandir Sahib without fail, and each year, she fed two orphans on Buddha Purnima.'

'How do you know all this?'

'Because I am her friend. I've been with her to the mandir many times. Last year, she came back here on Buddha Purnima.'

'Where is she now?' Mukesh asked.

'I told her that she could live with us and help us in the kitchen, but she didn't agree. She said that it would affect our friendship. So I got her a job as a cook in my cousin Gurpreet's house. He's a nice man and stays around forty kilometres from here. Since I've told him about her background, he looks after her well and is kind to her, but she also works sincerely in his house.'

Mukesh fell silent. He was sad that his mother worked as a cook in someone's home. The old lady said, 'Beta, you haven't touched your food at all! Please eat something.'

'May I have Gurpreet's address?' he asked instead.

'Sure, beta. I'll even tell him that you are going to visit him.'

Mukesh quickly gulped down the lassi and gobbled up a paratha before heading out to Gurpreet's home in a taxi. He was disillusioned. He thought that his parents would have done well in Punjab and had more children after he was gone. After all, he was the one who was thought to bring bad luck to the family. He was incredibly dejected about the state of his mother.

Mukesh looked out through the window. Dhabas, chicken shops, liquor stores, healthy crops and stout sardars joking around passed by in a haze. He saw trucks standing at every corner and women working in the fields. His mind barely recorded anything. In any other situation, he would have wanted to see more of Punjab's culture and learn about its agricultural industry. But he was in no mood today. The sun was bright and the world seemed to go on as usual.

He had no problem finding Gurpreet's address in the small village. The man was rich and everybody knew where he lived. The villagers pointed him to a house located between acres of fields, where he saw cows grazing. He stopped the taxi and walked to the house. He could hear the water flowing through the canals. As he approached the building, he realized that there were, in fact, two separate houses that shared an open kitchen in the centre. A tractor, a car, a motorcycle and a bicycle were parked on one side of the house and a Punjabi TV channel was playing at a high volume. The courtyard had charpoys laid out under the cool shade of a neem tree.

When he entered, a middle-aged man met him with a warm smile, 'I am Gurpreet. Chachi told me that you would be coming here today. Beta, Rupinder is like a *masi* to me. Please feel comfortable and think of this house as your own.'

Mukesh smiled back and nodded.

The man directed him to sit down and a young boy abruptly appeared with a big glass of lassi for the guest. Mukesh noticed that Gurpreet was dressed in his finest clothes, as if he were going to a wedding.

'Beta, I'm really sorry but I have to attend an important function,' said Gurpreet. 'My family has already left for the venue and I must leave immediately too, but we'll be back in the evening. Please stay with us for at least a week and relax here. I'll take you to the gurdwara tomorrow.'

Mukesh felt awkward. He was used to his parents' generosity, but this was too much. He stood up to say goodbye to his host, then sat down on the charpoy again after Gurpreet had left.

As the minutes ticked by, he felt anxious. It was time to meet his biological mother. What should he call her? Amma, Maaji or Rupinder? Suddenly, he heard footsteps and turned around. He saw a thin, old lady walking slowly towards him. She was wearing an ordinary salwar-kameez and her head was covered. She said softly, 'I heard that you want to see me, but I don't know who you are. What should I cook for you, beta?'

For a few seconds, Mukesh did not know what to say. He held back his tears and said to her, 'Please, sit down.'

She sat on the other end of the charpoy and asked, 'What's your name? And where do you come from?'

Mukesh was familiar with Hindi because of his flair for languages. He said, 'I heard that you lived in Jalna a long, long time ago. And you had a south Indian friend called Sumati. Do you remember her?'

Rupinder was taken aback. 'I can never forget her,' she replied.

'I'm her son.' He paused. 'Munna.'

She stared at him incredulously.

'I've come to see you.'

'I can't believe it.'

'My father died two weeks ago. That's when I learnt that I was not my parents' biological son. My mother never told me, maybe because she had promised you.'

Rupinder looked at him. Her little Munna was tall and healthy now. She was happy but did not say anything.

Mukesh said, 'I want to ask you something.'

'What is it, beta?'

'Parents usually don't give their children away unless it is a question of life and death. Even the poorest of the poor such as beggars want to keep their children. Then why did you give me away so easily? Didn't my father resist your decision? How could you be so hard-hearted that you never came to see me?'

'What did Sumati tell you?' Rupinder barely got the words out.

'Amma said that you were in a very difficult situation and that you really didn't have a choice. Your options were to leave me in a village with your parents or in an orphanage run by a gurdwara.'

She changed the subject, 'What does Sumati call you?'

'Munna. Everybody at home calls me Munna.'

Rupinder closed her eyes and took a deep breath, 'Even I used to call you Munna.'

Mukesh could not control himself, 'Just because I had a dark patch on my foot and your mother-in-law felt that it was a bad omen, how could you reject me without a second thought? Didn't my father ever want to see his child again?'

'Beta, for several years, I remembered you every single day. I wanted to leave everything and come to see you. And yet, I couldn't do anything.'

'Why? Why didn't you convince my father?'

Rupinder bowed her head and refused to answer him. Mukesh repeated the question. Finally, she lifted her head and said, 'Munna, you are my son. You are a part of my heart, even today. That's the truth. But your father didn't feel the same way and so it became easy for him to leave you.'

Suddenly, Mukesh grasped what she was saying. He collapsed on the charpoy.

'Then who is my father?'

8

The Innocence of Love

Rupinder was a young and strong girl from a very poor family. Her parents and brother were labourers in a zamindar's house. Whenever there was a wedding or langar in the village, she was always invited because she was helpful and friendly. Many suitors wanted to marry her, but when Surinder's family came from Jalna and proposed marriage to her, it was a matter of great celebration for her family. Surinder was handsome and his family appeared to be very rich. Immediately, her father agreed to the match and the wedding was conducted in Jalna. Rupinder felt sad about leaving her beautiful village in Punjab and cried bitterly.

When she reached Jalna, she realized in a few days that her life there was no different from the one she had left behind. In reality, her husband's family was not rich at all and she had to work all the time in their home—almost like an unpaid maid. Her mother-in-law dominated her and Surinder just watched from the sidelines. Soon, she became very lonely. At least she had had freedom in her village back home. Here, she had lost even that. She missed the fresh air, her she-buffalo, and her relatives and friends. Her attempts to become pregnant over two years failed miserably and her mother-in-law taunted her often. She held her responsible for not producing her son's heir. Then, unexpectedly, Rupinder became pregnant and started falling sick very often. Instead of helping out around the house, she became a burden to the family. One day, her mother-in-law said firmly, 'We can't look after you over here. You're only giving us more headaches. Go to your parents' village and come back after your delivery.'

Rupinder went happily but she did not stay at her parents' home. Her family was doing a little better financially and her brother had rented out a farm. The family stayed there and worked together in the fields, which were next to a mango grove managed by a watchman. The owner of the grove lived in Bombay and visited his property only once a year. One day, Rupinder's pink dupatta that had been left to dry in the fields flew with the wind and into the mango grove. When she went there to look for it, she realized that there was a small guest house inside the walls of the grove. She asked the watchman, 'Is someone living here?'

The watchman nodded, 'There is a young girl called Nirmala Kumari who's staying here temporarily because of her sickness. She has tuberculosis and has come here with her attendant Dulari.'

Rupinder loved to socialize and make friends. So she walked up to the guest house and introduced herself to Dulari, who was a middle-aged woman busy with her household chores. But Dulari was a woman of few words and they barely had a conversation.

Two days later, Rupinder went there again and asked Dulari about Nirmala. Dulari changed the subject and told her that Nirmala needed to rest and that she did not want to meet anyone.

After a week, Rupinder saw Nirmala for the first time. The sixteen-year-old was sitting in the veranda reading a book. When Rupinder approached the girl, she immediately understood why Nirmala did not want to meet anyone. She initiated a friendly conversation and the two women struck up a close friendship within a few weeks.

One day, Nirmala caught hold of Rupinder's hand and said, 'Please don't tell anyone about me.'

Rupinder knew what she was talking about. Nirmala was pregnant—just like her—and the two women were expecting to deliver within a month of each other. Nirmala did not want people in the village to know about her condition and that was why everyone was told that she was suffering from an illness. She told Rupinder, 'My husband has made me pregnant and left me. I'll give birth to the baby here and go back to my village.'

Rupinder realized that Nirmala was not telling her the truth, but she did not pursue the matter.

Two months went by. One evening, Rupinder went into labour. After a long and painful night, she delivered a stillborn baby. Immediately, her parents-in-law were informed about the tragedy.

Rupinder was overcome with sorrow. She knew that when she went back to her husband, she would have to hear her mother-in-law's sarcastic comments in addition to dealing with the loss of her baby and being overworked. Surinder had never been a companion or shown her any form of kindness. He did not care about her at all. When she had become pregnant after years of marriage, she had dreamt of a baby who would change her life—he would hold her hand and share her difficulties when he grew up. Maybe he'd be with her in old age too. But her dreams had been shattered into tiny little pieces; she refused to eat or drink and cried all the time.

Nirmala became concerned about her health. To distract her friend, she decided to share her story with Rupinder.

She said that her father was Choudhary Charan Singh, who was a big zamindar and the most powerful man in his village. He was a large-hearted but short-tempered man and viewed the world in black and white. People were either his friends or his enemies. He had two stepbrothers who loathed him and often taunted him, 'What's the use of all your land and money if there is no male heir to succeed you?'

The comment always irked Choudhary. He only had a daughter while his stepbrothers had two sons each. Choudhary thought about it and decided to marry his daughter into an influential family. Then his stepbrothers would not be able to pass any more comments.

His good friend, Lal Mohan, was a zamindar in a nearby village. If Nirmala married Lal Mohan's son, Brij Mohan, then that would make their position stronger in both their villages and they would have a better political future together. Choudhary had heard that Brij Mohan was soft on women and liquor but this did not bother him. It was common in their culture, after all. So he promised his friend that when the time came, Brij Mohan would become his son-in-law. Lal Mohan was happy with the alliance. Not only was Nirmala a good-looking girl, but his son would also get all the votes from Choudhary's village.

Meanwhile, Nirmala was blissfully unaware of her father's future plans and started studying at home by herself due to the absence of a high school in the village. Diligently, she worked day and night in preparation for her tenth class exams.

Time passed and seasons changed. Soon, it was winter.

One day, a young and handsome college student came to study the old monuments on the outskirts of the village for a history project, and rented out a room. When he went to buy some bananas, the shopkeeper told him, 'Why don't you go to Choudhary's house and talk to him? He'll definitely assist you if you need help with the project.'

When the young man met Choudhary Charan Singh, he was scared. The zamindar was a tall, hefty man with a big moustache and a perpetual scowl on his face. He asked the boy in an authoritative voice, 'Who are you?'

'I am Anand and I've come to your village for six months to work on a history project for my college. I'll be grateful if you would be kind enough to introduce me to somebody who can take me around the village or the areas nearby based on my project's requirements.'

'Where are you staying right now?'

'I'm staying in a *musafirkhana* near the Hanuman temple.'

Choudhary took pity on the young boy and said, 'Well, you can stay in my outhouse from tonight. Don't worry about food. We'll make sure that you get food every day.'

Anand was surprised by Choudhary's generosity and thanked him profusely. Soon, he settled into a routine. He left the outhouse every morning after breakfast and came back in the evening in time for dinner.

One day, he saw a girl applying mehendi on her hand in the backyard. She looked like she was a few years younger than him. There was something so attractive about her that he could not stop staring. When she saw him looking at her, she was startled and ran inside the house, leaving the mehendi behind. Anand went closer to where she had been sitting and saw a tenth-grade English textbook next to the bowl of mehendi. He realized that she must be the zamindar's daughter.

In the evening, Anand went and met Choudhary. He told him, 'Sir, I know English very well. If you'd like, I am available to teach the language to anyone who might be interested.'

Choudhary replied, 'We don't have a good English teacher in this village. In fact, there is no high school here either. So my daughter, who is in the tenth grade, is studying on her own. Why don't you teach her for as long as you are here?'

Anand nodded happily.

He started teaching Nirmala twice a week. At first, she was shy and awkward but, slowly, they became friends. Still, she completely ignored him when Choudhary was at home, and maintained a distance.

One day, Anand slipped during one of his monument expeditions and sprained his ankle. When Choudhary did not see him for three days, he asked Nirmala, 'Where is Anand these days?'

'I don't know,' she said.

Choudhary ordered the cook, 'Go right now and find out what's happened to the boy.' He turned to Nirmala and said, 'I would have asked your mother to do it but she's not yet back from her pilgrimage. I hope that the boy has eaten something in the last few days. I don't want anybody to go hungry in my house.'

When Choudhary learnt that Anand could not walk for a few days, he told his daughter, 'Ensure that he gets all his meals in his room.'

Nirmala nodded and diligently brought food for Anand three times a day. During one such visit at lunch, Anand touched Nirmala's hand as he took the food tray from her. At first, her hand shook a little. It felt new and different, but she did not push him away and accepted it shyly. Anand understood that she liked him too and they started spending a lot of time together after that.

9

A Journey Continued

Within a few months, Nirmala appeared for her exams and passed with flying colours. Choudhary thanked Anand and gave him an expensive gift before he left the village and went back to the city. That same month, Nirmala skipped her period and did not even notice. Soon, she started feeling nauseous; she thought that it was indigestion. After three months, she finally realized what was wrong with her. She recalled the two rifles decorating the family room and became frightened of what her father would say and do. What if he wanted to kill her? She had no idea that her relationship with Anand could result in a pregnancy!

Nirmala did not have the courage to tell her mother, nor did she have any friends who could keep her secret. But she trusted Dulari, the maid in the house. Somehow, she told Dulari the truth, who in turn conveyed the bad news to her mother. At first, her mother slapped and cursed her, before she sat down and burst out crying. That same evening, Dulari brought a herbal medicine from the local doctor to induce an abortion, but it did not help.

Now, Nirmala's mother had no choice but to tell her husband. Choudhary was livid and beat his daughter mercilessly. She had brought shame upon the family and he wanted to murder her; but since she was his only child, eventually common sense prevailed. Moreover, if he killed her, his hateful stepbrothers and their children would get his property and money. He was very upset with his wife for leaving their daughter unsupervised with Anand.

Choudhary thought about the problem for a few days and came up with a plan. He did not want Nirmala to marry the city boy; Anand was from a different community and belonged to a poor family. So Choudhary decided that he would give his daughter's baby away and then get her married to Lal Mohan's son, as planned.

But Nirmala was already starting to show. Choudhary did not want anybody to see her or know about the illegitimate child. He decided that it was time to send her somewhere far away for the delivery; she could come back after leaving the baby there. After a few days he told his wife, 'I have made all the arrangements. My cousin has an isolated farmhouse around two hundred kilometres from here, but he lives in Bombay. I've talked to him and told him that Nirmala is unwell and needs a change. So I will send her there with Dulari, but you will stay here with me. Otherwise, people may start doubting our story. Please tell Dulari about my instructions. I don't care if Nirmala gives birth to a boy or a girl. The child should be given away or left there. Nirmala must come back alone.'

'But . . .'

'Let me finish. It is Dulari's job to get rid of the baby. We will pay her handsomely for her silence. Once Nirmala is back, I'll get her married and we'll have a grand wedding.'

Three days later, Choudhary and his wife sent Nirmala and Dulari to the farmhouse.

~

When Nirmala ended her story, Rupinder felt grateful for the life she had.

Nirmala said sadly, 'At least you have a life ahead. But my future is not mine at all. How am I going to just throw my child away? And if I don't, I know for certain that my father will kill both of us. He's a very powerful man. There's no escape for me.'

'But my life is a desert too. My baby was supposed to be my oasis. He was the one who would have brought happiness into my life,' Rupinder countered.

That same evening, her thoughts turned towards Nirmala, 'She's going to return to the village after she gives birth, but where's she going to leave her baby?'

Suddenly, a thought struck Rupinder and she walked over to Nirmala's house.

Luckily, it was Nirmala herself who opened the main door. Rupinder blurted out, 'Will you give me your baby? It will give me someone to live for. I promise you that I will look after him very well.'

Nirmala was so taken by surprise that she stepped back and lost her footing. Rupinder rushed inside to help her to the nearest chair.

A few hours later, Nirmala's labour pains began. Between her painful contractions, she removed the gold chain from around her neck and gave it to Rupinder. She said, 'I know that you'll love my baby with all your heart. This chain is all that I've brought here with me, Rupinder. Please keep it and give it to my baby. Promise me that you'll take this secret to your grave.'

'I will. I won't tell anyone—not even the baby,' promised Rupinder.

Nine long hours later, Nirmala delivered a healthy baby boy in the wee hours of the morning. Exhausted, she held the baby tightly and then fell asleep.

Dulari wondered what they should do next.

Rupinder suggested, 'Leave the baby on the steps of the temple around seven in the morning. I'll pretend that I went there to pray and found the baby.'

Dulari nodded wordlessly and Rupinder went home.

Early in the morning, Nirmala saw her baby boy for

the last time. She cried and touched his feet, 'Beta, please forgive me. I didn't know how a child was born and I brought you into this world in my ignorance. I don't know what your future holds, but I can't just leave you somewhere to die of hunger or cold. Rupinder is a nice woman. At the very least, she'll ensure your survival and you won't grow up as an illegitimate child. I pray to God that no woman gets punished the way that I'm getting punished now.'

She closed her eyes and gave the baby to Dulari, 'Take him before I change my mind.' She added, 'Pack everything quickly. We're going back home in a few hours.'

As per plan, Rupinder went to the temple at seven. A crowd had already gathered around the abandoned baby and Dulari was keenly observing the drama from a distance.

Somebody asked, 'Who has left this baby here?'

People shrugged their shoulders.

'Which community is he from?'

'Has a woman in the village delivered recently?'

'Is the baby from another town?'

Nobody knew anything. Finally, an old man said, 'I was here outside the temple last night and saw a couple come in a car, but it was too dark to see anything else. Later, I tripped on the steps and thought that something was there, but I didn't bother to check.'

'Well, we can't just leave the baby here. Who's willing to take care of him temporarily?' a man asked.

Sensing her opportunity, Rupinder said sadly, 'My baby died a few days ago and I don't know what to do with myself. If you allow me, I would like to look after the baby. I'll stay here for at least a month and wait for someone to claim him. If nobody turns up, then I'll adopt the baby and take him with me to my husband's home.'

It was a good solution and everyone nodded in approval.

Rupinder picked up the newborn and hugged him. She sighed with relief, 'Munna, you are safe!'

Immediately, milk started filling her breasts and she ran home to feed the baby.

Rupinder waited for a month but as anticipated, nobody came forward to claim Munna. After another week, she went back to Jalna. Nobody came to pick her up from the railway station because Surinder's family was unhappy that she was bringing back an orphan with her. Conveniently, her mother-in-law blamed Munna's dark patch for the loss in the family's business and started treating him badly. Not surprisingly, Surinder also felt that the child should be sent back to where he came from or left in a gurdwara orphanage. Left with no suitable alternative to ensure a better future for Munna, Rupinder gave him to Sumati.

~

Mukesh felt like he was in a nightmare. He had never even considered the possibility that he might be an illegitimate child. Now he understood why Surinder gave him up so easily, why nobody came to see him or ever inquired about him. But Rupinder had saved him from being a child left in a garbage can, raised on the streets. She had brought him to Jalna and taken care of him for as long as she could.

Rupinder looked at him with love, 'Munna, God has punished me for my sins. I was never able to get pregnant after that one time. Sometimes I felt that I made a big mistake in letting you go. I should have kept you with me. But if I had done that, you would have been a coolie or a worker in somebody's house today. I wouldn't have been able to do what Sumati has done for you. How do I thank her for taking care of you so well?'

Mukesh was speechless. It was very hard for him to absorb that he was born out of wedlock and simply abandoned, that he was an unwelcome guest to this world. 'What am I supposed to do now? What kind of a journey have I been on—born somewhere and brought up as someone else? Who am I—a Hindi-speaking Jat, a Punjabi-speaking sardar or a Kannada-speaking south Indian? Or will Nirmala tell me another story?'

Rupinder went inside the house to bring food for him. When she came back, he asked, 'Where is Nirmala Kumari now? Do you have her address?'

'I don't know. But her husband Brij Mohan is a minister

in Delhi. I've seen them on television sometimes, but I don't have any contact with her.'

Mukesh did not ask her for more information.

He was unhappy seeing Rupinder's condition. His mother should not be working in her old age. The least he could do was to make her comfortable in this phase of her life. He told Rupinder, 'I'll send you money every month so that you don't have to cook for someone else. Please don't worry. The money I will send is my hard-earned money from London. I'll also talk to Gurpreet and buy a small house in Amritsar so that you can visit the gurdwara every day. Tell me, do you still feed orphans on Buddha Purnima?'

'Yes, beta, of course. You were born on that day. That's why I feed people in whatever capacity I can.' She paused. 'I didn't look after you with the expectation of you helping me in my old age. Wahe Guru has been kind and I still have some strength left. I can work and provide for myself. I don't need charity, Munna.'

'I am not helping you out of charity. It is a son's duty to care for his mother. You looked after me and I'm so glad that you did.'

Mukesh touched her feet, 'Please bless me so that I may reach the end of this journey and find myself.'

Rupinder smiled and placed her hand on his head.

10

The Final Stop

From the Amritsar railway station, Mukesh phoned his wife. 'Vasanthi, I need your help but I don't have much time to talk right now. How are you?'

'I'm all right. What do you need?' she asked immediately.

'How much money do I have in my bank account there?'

'Why?'

He was brief, 'I'll tell you later.'

Vasanthi replied, 'I think it's approximately one crore rupees.'

'The thing is . . . I want to write a cheque for sixty lakhs to someone,' he told her.

'Who?' she asked gently.

'I have to repay a debt, Vasanthi. Sorry, I have to go now. I'll call you later.'

Before she could ask any more questions, he said goodbye and hung up.

As the train started its journey, Mukesh felt like the wobbly bogies himself. The very thought of Nirmala upset him. How could she have been so irresponsible? She had gone back to her life after delivering a baby, and had not cared enough to find out how her son was. He felt cheated.

As he thought about her more and more, he recollected his television documentary about unwed mothers in India. The programme had been aired on BBC a few years ago. He himself had concluded that lack of sex education and job opportunities, and the strict norms of society made the life of an unwed mother and her child very difficult in India. But he'd never imagined in his wildest dreams that he himself was one of the children born of unwed mothers. Mukesh finally understood Nirmala's predicament and calmed down somewhat. Still, he was sad. He did not know why he wanted to meet her now but he knew that he had to.

After reaching Delhi, Mukesh surfed the Internet for information. Within half an hour, he learned that Brij Mohan was the minister for women and child development. He was married to Nirmala Kumari and had two sons, who were both in politics. One of his sons had been caught drinking and driving and the other had been accused of accepting bribes on behalf of his father.

Finally, Mukesh found what he was looking for—Brij Mohan's residence was on Prithviraj Road in south Delhi. Mukesh was easily able to trace his address and office phone numbers online, but knew that he would not be allowed to meet the minister without an appointment. The only way to meet him was through his media credentials. He would have to use his BBC background to gain entry into Brij Mohan's residence.

Mukesh dialled Brij Mohan's secretary's cell phone number. When the secretary answered, Mukesh introduced himself, 'Hello, I am Mukesh Rao. May I have a meeting with the minister, please?'

'No, he's extremely busy,' the secretary refused his request without a second thought.

'I work for BBC and want to interview the minister's wife for a TV series.'

Hastily, the secretary changed his tone, 'Of course, please come and meet the minister tomorrow at 8 a.m.'

The next day, Mukesh reached the minister's sprawling bungalow on time but was asked to wait in the visitor's lounge, which was already almost full of people. The minister's family was just waking up. While waiting, Mukesh observed the room he was in. It was disorganized and lavishly decorated with poor taste. There were plastic flowers in multiple vases in the room. A jade Buddha statue that had not been dusted for months stood in a corner and a painting of Lakshmi adorned with old and dry garlands was displayed near it. A dozen servants were moving in and out of the room serving tea, samosas and rasgullas to the visitors.

After an hour, Brij Mohan came to the visitors' lounge followed by his entourage who were carrying paan and files in their hands. The man was stout and short and dressed in a safari suit with his stomach bulging out. His eyes were swollen and it looked like he had had a late night. When they saw him, everybody stopped talking and stood up. Without looking left or right, Brij Mohan walked straight into the next room that had been converted to a large-sized office space.

Mukesh thought, 'Had Nirmala kept me with her, my fate would have been to become one of his entourage and carry paan and files for him; or if the minister had treated me like his own, I would have become another son getting into trouble with the law.'

After another hour, he was invited into the office room to meet the minister. When Brij Mohan saw his business card, he remarked, 'Ah! You're the London boy who wants to take an interview—not mine, but my wife's.'

'Sir, this particular piece is about how the wives of famous men spend their time supporting their husbands and their careers.'

'My wife does not speak English very well and she's very shy too. Why don't you ask me the questions and I'll try to answer them on her behalf?'

Mukesh was apologetic, 'No, Sir, please forgive me. It is my duty to talk to the women and report the interviews. I'll be happy to conduct the interview in Hindi.'

'Well, there really isn't much that she can tell you. My wife is a religious woman and spends most of her time in pujas. At other times, she accompanies me for appropriate events.'

'Then it shouldn't take much time, Sir. But I must talk to Ma'am.'

The minister shrugged his shoulders, 'That's no problem, but please remember to steer clear of controversial topics. Also, send us your article for approval prior to publishing.'

'Of course, Sir,' Mukesh nodded.

Brij Mohan called one of the servants and told him, '*Bachcha*, take him to Bibiji and tell her that I have sent him.'

Mukesh followed the servant to the main house. He entered a living room that had leather couches, a huge television set and some exotic artefacts. A huge picture of a popular Swamiji adorned one of the walls. From where Mukesh was standing, he could see a beautifully decorated puja room inside. The smell of incense was everywhere. The servant asked him to sit down while he went in search of Madam.

A minute later, a young boy appeared with tea, samosas and gulab jamuns, but Mukesh refused the food with a wave of his hand. He could not eat anything right now. He was about to meet Nirmala and suddenly felt nervous. A young man around his age came in with a cigarette in his hand and went into another room, without even glancing at him. 'Maybe he's one of Nirmala's sons,' Mukesh thought.

After a few minutes, a middle-aged woman dressed in a silk sari with the pallu over her head walked into the room and sat down in front of him. She said in chaste Hindi, 'Namaste, I am Mrs Nirmala Kumari, Brij Mohan ji's wife. I don't usually give interviews, but I've come because you insisted.'

Mukesh simply watched her. She was his mother—a mother who had abandoned him within hours of his birth, a mother who had conceived him without preparing for the consequences, a mother who thought that teenage sex was enjoyable but did not know that it would result in a pregnancy, a mother who was dominated by the men in her life.

He forgot what he had wanted to ask her.

Suddenly, there was a lot of noise outside the living room. Brij Mohan was leaving the house. He and his entourage got into six cars and drove away accompanied by an escort. The visitors poured out into the driveway and the lounge became vacant.

Mukesh heard the sudden roar of motorcycles and cars drifting further away, followed by an eerie quietness. A servant came in and told Nirmala, 'Bibiji, both the Chhote Sahebs have left with Bade Saheb. They'll be back at night.'

'Fine, then clear the dining table, please.'

The servant went away to follow her instructions.

Mukesh asked her, 'Ma'am, what are your hobbies?'

'I love reading. It is my childhood passion,' she answered simply.

'If you don't mind, may I ask you about your childhood?'

She nodded.

'Where did you go to school?'

'In my village. But I took private tuitions for my tenth class examinations since there was no high school there. After my wedding, I came to Delhi and completed a correspondence course.'

'Why didn't you go to college?'

She sighed, 'My parents-in-law were old-fashioned and preferred that I didn't go outside the home to study.'

Mukesh gathered up his courage and finally asked, 'Ma'am, do you remember Rupinder?'

Suddenly, Nirmala's eyes widened and her face became pale. She went out of the room to check if anybody was listening. Then she came back into the living room and closed the door. 'Which Rupinder?' she asked.

'The same woman who had a farm next to a mango grove. She's the one who gave me this gold chain.' Mukesh tugged on the chain around his neck.

He saw that she was too scared to respond, and yet she could not stop staring at him. He reassured her, 'Ma'am, please don't worry. I haven't come with any purpose except to meet my real mother.'

'Was Rupinder the one who told you everything?'

'Yes, she did, but only after I forced her to.'

'When?' she questioned him.

'Yesterday.'

'What?' Nirmala was puzzled. 'Didn't you know about it all these years?'

'No, I met her for the first time just yesterday.'

'Oh. If you weren't with her, then where were you?' she asked, concerned.

'God works in mysterious ways, Ma'am. He came to me in the form of Sumati and Krishna Rao. They became my parents and loved me as their own, gave me the best education that they could and built my self-confidence. I lost my father two weeks ago. That's when I found out that Rupinder had given me to them when I was a year and a half old.'

Nirmala started crying, 'Beta, you must be very upset with me. I couldn't do anything for you . . .'

'I am not upset with you, Ma'am. I am thankful that you gave me away to Rupinder, who gave me to Sumati. My curiosity to see my biological mother brought me here. I promise you that this secret will remain with me. But I also wanted to know about my father. Will you please tell me about him?'

She closed her eyes, 'I don't know where he is and I never tried to look for him. When I think of the past, it feels like a nightmare. Your father didn't even know that I was pregnant—and even if he did, my father would not have allowed us to get married.'

Nirmala gazed at him. 'Are you married?' she asked.

'Yes, I am. You brought me into this world and I am grateful, but I know that you won't like to keep in touch with me.'

Before she could reply, he touched her feet. He felt wet teardrops on his hair. She caressed his head with a shaky hand. He was her past—her first child. She choked on her words, 'I am happy that you've kept the chain with you till now. That's the only way I can remain with you in this life. I used to think that Karan and Kunti only existed in the Mahabharata, but now it's happened to me. My blessings and prayers will always be with you.'

When he stood up straight in front of her, she folded her hands and said, 'You must have heard about my children and their terrible reputation. It is better to remain childless than have bad children. You are far superior to them and I'm proud. Giving birth is simply a biological event but parents must move mountains to raise a child to be a good human being. I salute the mother who made you what you are.'

A moment later, Mukesh turned around and walked out of the house.

II

What Matters in the End

Mukesh never went in search of his biological father. There was no need any more. He must have settled somewhere in India with his children too. There was no place for Mukesh in his biological parents' lives.

Now Mukesh realized how much he missed his Amma. She knew him and loved him more than anyone else in the world. He was not a Jat or a sardar. He was a Brahmin from south India. He knew who he was now.

Mukesh took the next flight from Delhi to Bangalore and slept like a baby on the plane.

As he was walking out of the airport, he thought about Vasanthi. He had still not told her anything about what he was going through. This was something that had to be done in person. He hailed a cab and called her on the way home. 'If you are better now, can you please come to

Bangalore and be with me? I want to talk to you about something important,' he said.

Vasanthi was surprised. She said, 'Of course I'll come. In fact, I'll be there by tomorrow. I've been waiting for your call. Amma told me about your sudden trip to Amritsar. She's been checking on me every day since then to make sure that I was doing all right. Are you okay? Why did you have to go to Amritsar?'

Mukesh was gentle, 'Vasanthi, I'll answer all your questions once you are here, but don't worry. I am fine.'

When he reached his parents' house in the afternoon, there was a spring in his step and a smile on his face. He was home.

He entered the house and hugged Sumati tightly—like he'd never let her go. Ever since he'd turned twenty, he had started touching his mother's feet whenever he greeted her, but as a child, he had always hugged her. Today, he hugged her as if he was that small child again and said, 'Amma, in the last few days, I have learnt that you are the architect of my life. I am your son and Neeru is my sister. Nothing can separate us in this lifetime.'

Sumati was surprised. She kissed his head like she used to do when he was younger.

He declared, 'I'm hungry, Amma. Give me something to eat.'

She kissed him again and went to the kitchen to make rice and rasam. She knew that he loved rice and rasam.

Thirty minutes later, Neeraja also joined them in time for the meal.

Sumati asked her son, 'Munna, what did Rupinder say to you?'

He answered between mouthfuls of food, 'Vasanthi will be here in the morning tomorrow. I'll tell all of you the whole story once and for all, Amma.'

His mother ruffled his hair and nodded.

Half an hour later, he went to his bedroom and fell asleep at once.

~

After Vasanthi reached early the next morning, Mukesh described his entire trip to his mother, sister and wife. Sumati was speechless—she herself had not known that he was Nirmala's son. In the end, they all agreed that the secret would stay with the four of them.

A few hours later, Mukesh and Vasanthi found themselves alone. She had not said much to him since she had learnt the truth in the morning.

Mukesh knew that she needed some time and told her, 'Vasanthi, you were married to me thinking that I belonged to your religion and community. I really don't know what you think of me right now. If you still want to be with me, I'll be the luckiest guy on earth. But if you think that it is too much for you to handle, I'll back off and respect your wishes on what you want to do next. I won't fight you.'

Quietly, he walked out of the room.

Vasanthi sat without moving. A few minutes passed and she tried to get her thoughts together. Mukesh was a great husband. He encouraged her to learn new things, loved her unconditionally and constantly tried to make her happy. It didn't matter what community he belonged to. It may make a difference to her father, but not to her.

She stood up and went to search for him. She found him standing outside on the balcony gazing at the sky. Silently, she came up from behind, touched his shoulder and put an arm around his waist. 'You may be anybody's son but you'll always be my husband,' she said.

Acknowledgements

An affectionate thank you to my trusted editor, Shrutkeerti Khurana, for the wonderful work and late-night sessions filled with creativity and fun.

Thank you, Udayan Mitra, for the constant support and belief in me.